The Demon & the Dryad

AN ARCANA GLEN SWEET PARANORMAL ROMANCE

TAROT ELF FANTASY MAJOR ARCANA SERIES
BOOK EIGHT

TARA MAYA

Welcome to Arcana Glen

Welcome to Arcana Glen, a magical town hidden in the Rocky Mountains of Colorado....

Here arcanes of all types are free to be themselves... Elves, Witches, Shifters, Seraphs, Dragons and more.

But until the Twenty-Two Guardians are restored to power, the Elven War rages among the arcanes. What's the solution?

True Love, of course!

To read a free love story and sneak a peek at what happened before the Massacre of the Guardians, ten years ago, CLICK HERE to sign up for the newsletter for Tara's Tribe and receive the free novella, ***The Genie & the Gymnast.***

The Genie & the Gymnast

FREE NOVELLA

THE GENIE

Jay Zee is a Jinn. He knows better than to grant wishes to humans. But he makes an exception in exchange for a shot at his dream job: working for the Magician. He never expects the old man to demand that Jay Zee marry his daughter...or that she is the most hideously ugly woman on Earth. As a terrible danger closes in on all of them, Jay Zee starts to question what is most important ... but it may be too late to stop a massacre.

THE GYMNAST

To her friends in the Enchanted Circus, Janet seems like a pretty, young, carefree performer. Even among other arcanes, she has to keep the secret of her true nature. Janet can't believe that her father forced her into marriage with a Jinn. She knows her new husband loathes her, but she can't help but dream that he might look past her twisted exterior.

This tale is a stand-alone HEA love story set ten years before most of the stories from Arcana Glen, on the eve of the Massacre of the Guardians.

Click here to join Tara's Tribe of Readers to and receive the latest news on more romantic fantasy stories and read The Genie and the Gymnast.

Email: editor@misquepress.com to request a free Review Copy of any of Tara Maya's novels.

About This Book

Naya found him injured in the forest.

Naya is a Dryad and a Healer. She also owns a water mill and forested land in Colorado. When she finds a stranger who needs her help, she offers it, no questions asked.

She has no idea that the gorgeous stranger is really a Demon Prince.

To win back his place in hell, Vass has to steal Naya's land... and her soul.

Pretending to be an ordinary shifter, he gets a job at her water mill. He's stolen a magic truck that enables him to erase any mistakes, so it should be easy.

He never counted on falling for the woman he was trying to seduce.

Welcome to Arcana Glen, a magical town hidden in the Rocky Mountains of Colorado....

Here arcanes of all types are free to be themselves... Elves, Witches, Shifters, Seraphs, Dragons and more.

Warning: This book deals with issues of addiction and uses stronger language than most Arcana Glen books.

One

August 5, 2022, Friday
First Quarter Moon

NAYA FAIRCHILD HUMMED along with the song of the trees as she walked through the mountain forest that she loved. Pine and fir, aspen and birch, she knew them all. Not only by various species did she recognize them; each individual tree was known to her by name. Many of them she had seen grow up from saplings. She had known their parents, and in some cases their grandparent trees. She knew which trees were alive with only a gentle vegetable quiescence and which were lively with a sentient spirit that indicated a true Hamadryad—an awakened, conscious tree, often the companion of a Dryad.

Her own companion tree, for instance, was an Aspen Hamadryad named Quigley Quiverbark. He played a similar role in augmenting Naya's magic that an animal Familiar played for a Witch; and like a Familiar, he was as wise and compassionate as any human could aspire to be, and far wiser and more compassionate than most humans bothered to be.

Naya protected the forest from humans. Humans would see only things to be cut and sawed and used. Naya saw a community. There were many Hamadryads, tree familiars, of her fellow Dryads here in these woods. The woods were also home to other magical creatures which had originally come from a distant mystical realm, the Sphere of Autumndelle, just like Naya and Quigley. Others who lived here and worked for her were from Springvale, another magical Sphere; and of course, there were also a large number of Animal Shifters, whose ancestors hailed from Winterdom. Most of the arcanes had lived for many years or even generations in the Mundane Sphere.

It was unusual for so many arcanes to live together in a human community, but Arcana Glen, a tiny town nestled in the Rocky Mountains, was a unique place.

Naya was not a stranger in the human community, any more than she was in the arcane community. She served as the bridge between the two.

In fact, to the surprise of many of the other Dryads, she ran her own timber company. In other words, she beat the humans at their own game, being the first to decide which trees to cut and harvest. She had a Timber Mill over the river, along with a lumberyard where the logs were cut into planks of specialty high-quality woods that she sold all over Colorado.

Of course, Naya protected Hamadryads, the sentient trees, from being accidentally treated like ordinary trees. She protected them from ax, chainsaw, or fire. As for the mundane trees, she loved them too, and was a good steward of their community. She knew that tempering excess growth was key to healthy forests, but she never over-cut her forest. She kept her eye on the future as well as on the past and ensured that she did not forget to replant saplings in the sunlit patches opened up by the removal of older growth. As long as she was here, in charge of the timber company on this mountain side, her forest would endure and survive and flourish.

Today, Naya ended her walk through the woods at the place where her own tree familiar grew. Quigley resembled a classic Colorado aspen, with a beautiful silvery trunk and yellow and orange leaves. Mundane aspens changed into their fall raiment over a little more than a week, sometime in late September or early October. But since Quigley was an arcane tree from Autumndelle, he donned his crown of golden leaves early in August and clung to them well after the snow fell.

Other than his unusual retention of autumn glory, when Quigley was asleep (which was most of the time), he was indistinguishable from an ordinary aspen. However, when he awakened, his face showed in the black marks on his white trunk. Quigley could not take a human form, but his bark face was quite expressive. Humans would not be able to tell the difference between the two kinds of trees, even though when Quigley was awake it was as obvious as the difference between a live human and a manikin.

Naya in her tree-blend form looked a lot like her tree. In her human form, she had sun tanned skin, golden hair, ears that swooped up and away from her face and were much longer than elven ears but not as furry as those of a fawn or satyr.

When Naya came into the vicinity of her tree friend, she softly called his name. He roused himself out of a deep sleep. The random pattern of black splotches on his white trunk shifted and transformed into the unmistakable features of eyes, eyebrows, nostrils, and mouth. He smiled to see her, slowly blinking away his nap.

She pressed her hands together and bowed to her friend.

"Namaste, Quigley!" she said. "Please accept my blessings and bless me in return. May you have wind in your branches, water in your trunk, light on your leaves, and mushrooms in your roots. May you grow in peace and be tall and strong and may you always love as much as you are loved."

"Thank you for your blessing, Naya, and accept my blessings in return," Quigley rumbled in a deep voice. He looked a little less dignified than usual because the Hamadryad had been asleep, and he yawned as he spoke. "May you have wind in your hair, mushrooms in your soup, water in your cup. May you grow in peace and be tall and strong and may you always love as much as you were loved."

He yawned again. Some Hamadryads, like some trees, were hermaphadites, but

Quigley was dioecious; he produced only male flowers, so she called him a "he-tree."

"How are you doing this morning my friend?" Naya teased. "A little sleepy, it looks like."

"You know how these summer mornings make me drowsy," he admitted.

Naya was about to pour the water from her handmade ewer over the roots of her friend, but the tree visibly shuddered and drew back.

"No, Naya, this morning I need water from a special part of the river. I need you to go all the way up to the Miqwe Falls and gather water from the pool, there."

"A strange request. Why?"

But Quigley had fallen back asleep.

Naya sighed. Quigley wanted her to hike halfway around her territory... in fact the pond was right at the edge of her lands that she owned... just to get special water? Naya knew that the magical properties of the river could change depending on what part of the land it flowed through. But her tree was usually not so picky. Always before, she would draw water from a healthy spot where the water was fresh and clear and full of healthy minerals and that would satisfy him.

But if Quigley wanted special water, he wouldn't change his mind or explain himself. She might as well fetch the water for the Hamadryad. There was no point arguing with a tree.

~

August 5, 2022, Friday
First Quarter Moon

Stupid, stupid trees. Trees everywhere tripped him up and slowed him down as he tried to run.

Once, not long ago, Vassily Glug'ulgros had been a Prince among demons, feared and honored by the minions of Darkpyre.

Now, he was a fugitive.

Vass ran like hell through the forest, cursing the trees in his way. He had only recently returned to human form and already he was being hunted. Flashbacks made it worse, jumbled memories of running on four legs, trapped in the form of prey animal, while predators snapped at his feet. Dry mouthed but sweating, Vass fought the urge to panic and fight, to turn around and charge with his tusks forward, like a boar.

Fortunately, the man hunting him was driving a huge monster truck, which had even more trouble making it through the screen of trees than Vass did on foot. Unfortunately, the truck was driven by Chet, an ex-demon who had switched to the Other Team, so to speak, and had a beef with Vass.

Chet's truck was actually a *Merkavah*, a chariot from heaven, which could take the form of any vehicle, and which, more importantly, had the ability to rewrite the day that had just passed for a do-over. That meant that Chet could keep hunting Vass over and over, until Chet found a version of today when Vass was caught.

Vass could not even remember the previous version of today, when, he presumed, he must have escaped. He only knew from certain telltale signs, because he also had some experience rewriting Time, that the day had already been reset at least once—perhaps more times. Only the Charioteer, the driver of the Chariot, would know for certain.

What Vass knew was that this morning, as soon as he woke up, already Chet was waiting with his truck, and a gun, screaming at him. Vass had no idea how Chet had found him. Perhaps a thousand days had passed when Chet had looked for Vass in vain. But Chet kept redoing yesterday until he got the outcome he wanted. He was a maniacal soma'a'vitch, and he was determined to kill or capture Vass.

In his haste, Vass almost ran off a cliff. Vass wheeled backwards. Below, he saw a tributary of the river that cut through these mountains. The water here was white, the current strong, and the incline was steep. He tried to run along the edge of the cliff, but something invisible pushed back on him. He recognized the energy of a magic shield.

Vass cursed in his own harsh demonic tongue. He must be near the Timber Mill. All of the forests on the slopes around the mill were owned by a timber company and protected by fierce magic explicitly designed to keep demons like him out of the territory.

He flailed around, trying to avoid both the cliff and the magic shield. The trees blocked the truck from his view right now, but he could hear the noisy engine revving closer.

Suddenly, something snapped around Vass's leg like jaws of steel. Vass screamed in pain and fell to his knees. He had stepped into a hunter's trap just like a deer or a wild boar.

He was convinced that Chet had set the trap. That damn trap was not meant for an animal. Woven into the steel was silver and magic designed to trap an arcane. It also poisoned him and made it impossible for him to remove.

Behind Vass, the monster truck had time to maneuver through the trees and park. Chet slid out and ambled over to him.

Vass glared at his former friend. Back in April, Vass had fought Chet once before, in the mountains not far from here, at some old farmhouse. The farmhouse had happened to be adjacent to a secret military base where the Dark Triad had established a foothold. The Dark Triad led an alliance of Winter Elves, Goblins, Ice Giants, and Demons; they hoped to secretly extend the war between the Spheres into the human realm.

A former Demon Warlord, Chet had once been part of that grand project, until the bastard betrayed the other demons and became a Guardian. There were Seven Mortal Spheres and Three Immortal Spheres in all, and the Guardians were the magical protectors of the Gates between all ten Spheres. The Guardians *pretended* to be neutral, but they weren't. Since the war effort required that the Dark Triad blast through the Gates to conquer all the Spheres, the Guardians were inevitably opposed to the war aims of the Dark Triad.

Chet smiled as he bore down on Vass. Vass scrambled back on all fours, with the f*king trap still around his leg, until once more he reached the edge of the cliff.

If I throw myself into the river, maybe the current will carry me past the shield, thought Vass. Maybe the shield will keep out Chet as well. After all, he may be a Guardian now, but he was born a demon!

The magic in the shield was an admixture of Stone and Water magic. Simple, hearty, Elemental magic, nothing fancy, and yet as a demon, he had never been able to operate here. What if the same applied to his friend and his magic truck?

There had to be a reason that his former friend drove him into a hunter's trap here at the edge of the magical, shielded land.

Chet reached him. It was too late for Vass to save himself. Chet could kill him now. Then Vass's spirit would return to Darkpyre, which was actually part of the Seven Lower Mortal Spheres, but which humans referred to as Hell. Which told you everything you needed to know about what a great place it was to live. Vass had been born and raised there, and at least he had been a prince, the son of one of the seven Demon Kings who ruled Darkpyre, so he had lived a life of spoiled luxury. But, if he returned there now, as a failure, as a disembodied spirit, his soul would probably be reborn as one of the millions of toiling slaves who worked in the factories and mines that serviced the great Infernal Machine.

The Infernal Machine was not really a machine. Some called it the Great Beast. But it was not really an animal. Some called it a collection of ancient and nameless primordial Dark Gods, gods of darkness and hatred, but it was not really a pantheon. It was Hunger personified, a great maw, and it had to be fed the souls of the damned, or it would consume everyone in Darkpyre.

I don't want to be reborn as a slave in the bowels of the great Infernal Machine, thought Vass. Anything is better than that.

"I don't want to kill you, Vass," Chet said. He might have been more convincing if he hadn't been aiming a gun at Vass's head.

"Why not?" sneered Vass. "Has going over to the other side really made you that much of a pussy?"

"It figures that's how you would see it," growled Chet. "I'm trying to give you a chance to change your life and better yourself. I know it's hard for you to give up the privileges you have as a Prince of Hell, but the price you pay is not worth it in the end. I think you are a good man at heart, but you have to reject the values of your father. Let me and the other Guardians help you."

Vass wanted to laugh. His old friend was trying to suborn him. Maybe he had a chance to escape after all.

"Would you really help me?" Vass asked, trying to project the right amount of doubt and hope. He feared his ruse was completely transparent, but he tried to make sincerity throb in his voice. The fact that he was still in pain from his leg helped make him sound agonized. He knew that his old friend would be able to sense a lie, so he stuck as much to the truth as possible. He chose each word carefully.

"I feel trapped, Chet. I'm in pain. You know what happened to me recently. I was transformed into an animal and my so-called friends, the ones that I grew up with, the other princes and Lords of Hell, took advantage of my weakness to humiliate me."

"They're not really your friends," said Chet. "They're just users. But you were a user too, Vass. I know you used magic like my Chariot, the infernal version, to enjoy the same feast in the pit of Tartarus over and over while tormenting starved prisoners. Every time you consumed the food of Hell, you grew more addicted to the dark magic that comes out of the Infernal Machine. You're worse off than a human cokehead right now. You can't live without it. The pain you're going through right now is withdrawal symptoms. But this is also an opportunity for you. You can reject all of that and start your life over."

"I am afraid to do that," said Vass. That was 100% the honest truth. He pointed to the magic-laced steel trap. "Can you get this damn thing off me? If you're not going to kill me, can we talk like two mature adults?"

"No," said Chet, infuriatingly, "Because I don't trust you. But I'm going to take you back to the Castle. Someone will remove the trap there."

Back at the Castle owned by the Magician, the most powerful Wizard in the Seven Mortal Spheres, there would be absolutely no chance to escape the dungeon of the Magician. No way was Vass going there if he could help it.

He grimaced and pretended to agree. "I know you don't trust me, and I know I've betrayed you before. I don't deserve another chance, but I'm begging you. I really do want to change. This time I really do want to get better..."

"I can't get up," he added pathetically.

Looking wary, his old friend came closer to him. Chet put his arm under Vass's shoulder and helped him to his feet.

Vass deliberately stumbled so that both of them were dragged closer to the cliff. He cried out in pain to disguise his strategy. When his friend looked down at his leg, an automatic response to Vass's flailing, Vass suddenly spun around, trying to grab the gun. Chet countered, but Vass kicked the metal trap on his foot into his friend's face, knocking Chet to the ground. Chet shot at him, but Vass evaded the bullet with superhuman demon speed. Vass tackled Chet, once again trying to grab the gun.

The two of them started grappling and wrestling. The Guardian was stronger, but Vass was filled with desperate need and hate. Chet was right about one thing. It had been too long since Vass had any food from his homeland, and he was feeling withdrawal pains like a modder'f'ker. He needed his magic back. He needed to eat. Mundane food tasted like sawdust to him. He needed power. He would do anything to get it, anything at all.

Drawing on a burst of brute strength, Vass shoved Chet over the cliff. Then Vass ran on his bum leg to the truck. He had to use his left foot because the right one was still a bloody stump trapped in the steel jaws, and every movement hurt.

When he tried to drive the truck further into the forest, he came up against the same invisible shield that had stymied him before. Light flared at the front of the truck and then he saw nothing but clear air between the trees. He was right. There was a spell protecting the forest, and it wouldn't allow the truck to drive through. But he had an idea. Often shield spells had a weak spot, something so crude the spell didn't anticipate it.

He got out of the truck. His leg protested, but he pushed past the pain. He went behind the truck and physically pushed it over the boundary.

The shield did not stop him.

On the other side, Vass climbed back into the truck and tried once again to drive. If the shield spell operated everywhere within the space, he wouldn't be able to drive it either, but if it was just a barrier then...

The truck revved up.

"Yes!" shouted Vass, pumping the air with his fist.

He drove it as deep into the forest as he could. But eventually, pain and exhaustion overtook him, and he passed out. The truck was on a slope, and it kept heading downhill, going faster and faster toward the river.

Two

August 5, 2022, Friday
First Quarter Moon

NAYA COULD WALK QUICKLY when she needed to. She could not actually fly, but she could flow as fast as a river over the land, seeking out all the low spots, working with the terrain rather than against it. Her light, skipping steps quickly brought her to the spot in the river that her tree had requested.

To her amazement, just as she arrived, she saw a huge pick-up truck, the kind that many of her workers used to haul wood and rocks, careen down the hill, headed toward the river. Naya realized it was going to splash into the river and possibly drown whoever was inside. She could see there *was* an occupant, although he appeared to be passed out. Normally, the shield around her forest kept out intruders, whether mundane or arcane. How had he smuggled his truck in here? Her spell particularly kept out any heavy machinery or vehicles because she didn't like them driving around her forest, scarring the trees and crushing the shrubs. Either a powerful counterspell had brought him here—or for some reason the forest spirits and the river goddess had decided to allow him in.

To stop his truck hitting the water and risk him drowning, she activated her dual powers of Elemental Stone and Water. She pushed the edge of the river back, while at the same time, she lifted the dirt and rocks on the path of the truck so that it created a curve in the other direction. The car rolled up this and then rolled back down and came to a rest at the bottom of a U-shaped cup of dirt.

Naya ran to the driver's side of the truck and found an unconscious man. He was a gorgeous specimen, notwithstanding that his clothes were filthy, and his right leg was caught in a nasty trap. She pulled him out of the car. Using waves of Elemental Stone and Water to help her convey his weight, she maneuvered him to the banks of the river. Was this why Quigley had requested water from this pool? Had her Hamadryad anticipated that this man would need her help?

Naya first rinsed his injury in the river. Next, she tried to unlock the trap, but she quickly saw that the trap was designed to ensnare an arcane. That made her frown.

Who would do such a thing? And who would dare do it on *her* land?

She knew there was a military base not far from her protected area. She hated those scum. They trapped Shifters. And possibly worse. If the dark conspiracy theories were true, there was a secret laboratory at the base, where sadists performed foul experiments on innocent arcanes in the bowels of the mountain. Naya had helped some of the Shifters who had escaped from there, so she did not dismiss the stories, although she had never seen the laboratory herself.

Obviously, the injured man was an arcane, probably a Shifter. An enemy had endeavored to trap him, but he had escaped. The forest must've allowed him in to help him because he was a good man fleeing evildoers. Not that it mattered. He was injured and Naya always helped those who were injured and helpless, no questions asked.

She bathed the dirt from his face and his body, although at this point, she did not remove his clothes. She still needed to take him back to her house to fully treat him.

Still, she could not help but notice how incredibly handsome he was. Like most Shifters, he was incredibly physically fit, or had been at one time. Right now, his body showed signs of starvation and abuse. Nonetheless, even that could not completely hide the fact that he had once been muscular and sleek. His hands were soft with no calluses. Interesting. Whatever work he had done, it wasn't the kind they did around her mountain. Even Naya, who had softer hands then most of her workers, still showed some signs of her outdoor labors. This man had the velvet smooth fingertips of an office worker whose heaviest machinery was a keyboard.

His face was almost *too* gorgeous. Men should not have such long lashes, she thought. But his cheekbones and his jaw were well defined and masculine. She wondered what color his eyes were. His hair was deep brown like the earth that she loved. It was filthy at the moment, but when she washed the dirt out, the short curls turned smooth and silky under her fingers. She blushed and realized that she had been caressing a man who was unconscious and needed her help. Where were her healers' instincts? She needed to get this man back to her home, where she had a spare room for patients who came to her for healing.

He was much too heavy for her to carry, and she couldn't use her Elemental magic the entire way back to her house. She was at the edge of her territory as it was.

She glanced at the truck. Fortunately, she knew how to drive, and in fact she had a pick-up truck of her own. Her bias against machinery was not as extreme of that of many Dryads. In fact, she had nothing against machines as such. Everything, when used in moderation, could be good. It was only when something was used to excess, out of balance with nature and with no respect for conservation for the future, that a thing became evil and dangerous.

~

August 6, Saturday
Waxing Gibbous Moon

Vass woke up in a tiny but picturesque room. Everything around him looked hand-crafted, even the river stone walls of the building itself. The cot was made of hand carved wood, the mattress, he could have sworn was stuffed with old-fashioned goose down, and the pillows as well. All of the sheets and the curtains on the window, which matched, were hand sewn and hand embroidered. The blankets were either unique quilts or hand crocheted out of real wool, not polyester. The one wall that was not made of rocks, the inner wall of the room, was white plaster painted with quirky little hand-painted murals of trees and woodland creatures.

A handcrafted chair had been placed next to the bed, but there was no one seated there. On a bureau rested a ceramic bowl, the kind that would have been used as a sink in the Nineteenth Century. Perhaps it *was* the sink; it was filled with clean, fresh, clear water, with rose petals floating in it. There were a few glass bottles next to the porcelain sink, hand lotions and other mysterious items. There was a bar of soap, also handmade, wrapped in a ribbon.

Vass had been raised in palaces and chateaus his whole life. Whether in Darkpyre or on Earth, he was used to being surrounded by the best, most expensive luxury items and artwork by famous modern artists. Usually, the work of the artist was abstract, angry, and deliberately perverted the ordinary values held by most people as a supposedly bold statement of the artist's defiance of convention. But he had seen so many similar supposedly bold, defiant-of-convention artworks, that to him, it was all conventional.

This immature folk style was something he would normally turn his nose at. Whoever made all this stuff was not an artist in any sense the High Art world would recognize. This kitsch would never sell in a gallery. It had been made for *this* room, *this* house, for the enjoyment of the artist who created it, and the enjoyment of the person in the room, with no larger scheme in mind, no political motive, no bold statement decrying the middle class and sneering at traditional morality. The little creatures on the wall were cheesy and cliché and not even that well drawn.

He tried to sneer but failed.

Sneering was too much work. He lay back on his feather pillow and stared at the ceiling. Even the ceiling had been decorated. It was all white, but swirls and patterns had been etched into the white plaster. Again, it struck him that every section of the room had been touched with a creative and loving spirit.

It was a powerful form of magic he had never experienced. The very air here felt healing to him. It was clean and fresh and scented with wildflowers. It was as if every part of the room was giving him a hug. He wanted to resist it, but he was too tired. He felt sick to his stomach, and he had a headache, and his leg throbbed.

His leg! It was only then Vass remembered his fight with his old friend, that traitor, Chet. Vass remembered pushing Chet off the cliff, remembered stealing the truck, pushing it into the shielded part of the forest. Vass remembered being in great pain as he tried to drive the truck with an injured leg still trapped in the steel and silver jaws of the animal trap.

Although he was still exhausted, he forced himself to sit up. The blanket bundled at his waist. He was almost naked. Someone had removed all his old clothes and put some new boxers on him. Well, wasn't that interesting. Who had been ogling his naked body? He examined his injured foot. He could still see the raw scars, but it had healed. And obviously someone had removed the trap.

He heard a woman singing. He froze. The sound was so sweet and innocent that he was disappointed when it ended, even though the door opened and the woman herself entered the room. She was illuminated by the sunlight from the window. He had never seen such a beautiful woman, not even compared to all of the succubuses and vampires and seductresses in Darkpyre, nor with all the top models and actresses and professional call girls that he had screwed in his lifetime.

Ash blonde hair fell down her back to her waist. She had one green eye and one brown. Her skin was tan but glowed with golden, healthy sheen. But it was her smile that lit up her entire face and the grace with which she moved that struck him most. She was like the beauty of the river in the forest, of flowers in spring, and the leaves in autumn, all wrapped up into one woman. He was stunned and instantly aroused. The blanket lifted with the evidence of his attraction.

He had never been embarrassed around a woman before, but he had never been around a woman like her before. He did not want to let her know his reaction, so he smoothed down the blanket and adjusted his position to hide his arousal.

~

Naya did not expect to find her patient already awake. Even for a Shifter, he must have immense stamina. The injury had not looked that bad, but that was not accounting for the poison in the trap. Not only silver, but some form of magic she could not identify infected him. All she knew was that it was not any form of Elemental magic; she knew the characteristics all of four Elements, although she only used two. Plus, he seemed to be suffering from withdrawal from some kind of drug. That made her think that her theory that he had escaped from the military laboratory was correct. She knew they used drugs and other horrible substances on the Shifters there.

When she entered, he flinched and stared at her with wariness and suspicion, more indications that he had gone through some terrible trauma. He was also sitting up when he should have been laying down sleeping. The look he gave her made her blush.

She had thought that she had gotten over her physical attraction to him. When she brought him to her house and changed him in the patient room, she was able to maintain a professional focus on healing his injury. But now that he was sitting up and she had a good view of his muscular chest, not to mention the obvious strong physical reaction he had to her, she felt an unexpected flush of desire in response.

She had healed many Shifters, many of them strong and handsome men, and many of them had responded physically to her just as he had. But this was the first time Naya herself had reacted so strongly in response. There was something about him, the combination of obvious strength and the vulnerability he tried so hard to hide, that tugged at her.

She had a weakness for a damaged man. It had not led to a healthy dating life. Sometimes a man was *too damaged*, and she could not bring him back from the brink.

Be careful, girl, she warned herself. Obviously, this man has been fighting demons, and you don't know if he's going to win or surrender to them. You can't save everyone.

"Where am I?" he demanded harshly. "Who are you? Am I a prisoner?"

He broke her heart with that last question. *Am I a prisoner?* He asked that as if it were the most natural thing in the world.

"Does this look like a prison to you?" she gestured to the open window.

"You were hurt, so I brought you here to heal you. You're still not completely healed. I would like to look at your leg, check if the poison had completely been drained from your system, and continue my healing. That trap was devious, but I believe I can fix you."

His lips twisted into a cynical smile. "I don't think you can fix me, Beautiful, but you're welcome to try."

Dammit. He was definitely her type. Totally broken and he knew it, yet still flirted and made light of his own pain. It made her want to brush his hair back from his forehead and tell him everything was going to be all right. At the same time, she knew that he was the type who would push her away because being with him would put her in danger or some stupid nonsense like that. That was when she had finally broken up with Riley. He refused to let her in. It was Riley who had taught her the hardest lesson of her life. *You can't save everyone.*

She looked at him with a silent plea. Please, she thought, let me help you. You don't have to do this alone. But you have to meet me halfway.

He jerked back as if he had heard her thoughts. He grew even more wary. She wondered if he possessed telepathy. It was a form of Psychic magic, not Elemental magic, but some Shifters possessed that as well. Especially those that had been experimented on. Naya did not usually guard her thoughts. She didn't think anything she wasn't willing to say out loud. Normally. But she realized that around this man, some of her thoughts might get downright embarrassing and she built a shield around them.

He grew even more wary. That confirmed it. He was *strongly* telepathic if he felt it the minute she raised her mental shields to keep her thoughts private. But he only flashed her a slow, roguish smile. He didn't comment on it out loud.

"Where is my truck?" he demanded.

"Parked outside. You're at my house. By the watermill."

"I want to leave."

"You can leave anytime you want," she said. "But it would be better if you let me finish healing you."

"Why should I trust you?"

She walked to his side, picked up his hand, and pressed his warm palm between both of her own. She looked him in the eye.

"Listen," she said. "It doesn't matter who you are. It doesn't matter what you are. It doesn't matter what powers you have. It doesn't matter what others have done to you. It doesn't matter what you have done to others. As long as you are here with me, you are safe. I will do my best to heal you. Whenever you want to leave, you can. But you don't have to run. I will not hurt you. That is my pledge to you. As a healer, I would never harm anyone in my care."

Three

August 6, Saturday
Waxing Gibbous Moon

THE SOUND OF HER WORDS, her sweet but firm voice, was almost like a song although her words were prosaic. The feel of his hand sandwiched between her soft palms made his skin flush. She created a wash of light and warmth that swept throughout his body.

Vass jerked his hand away from her, fearing that her touch was casting a spell over him. It certainly wasn't helping his arousal problem.

"That's a dangerous policy," he told her harshly. "You have no idea who I am. You could be helping a demon for all you know."

"I told you," she said, "It doesn't matter to me. What matters is that you're hurt, and you need help."

"Why put yourself in danger like that? It's a stupid policy to help someone who might turn on you."

"Are you going to turn on me?" She lifted her eyebrow archly. He lost himself in her eyes, the green and the brown, a perfect match even though they were nothing alike. He tried to swing himself out of the bed and a jolt of pain ripped through his body. He clenched his teeth.

She gently touched his bare chest. "Please," she said. "Lie down. Let me help you."

Those were the same words she had been thinking when he tried to probe her mind. He had never met someone whose inside was so congruent with their outside. He had never met someone with nothing to hide.

He rejected that idea as soon as he saw it. *Everyone* had something to hide. Everyone had some sin, some vice, some weakness. Everyone had some addiction you could exploit. He just had to find hers. Maybe her weakness was just what it seemed. Her willingness to take care of anybody, even a wretch like him. Despite her claim, he suspected that if she ever found out the truth of what he was and what he had *actually* done in his life, all her sweet words would fly right out that open window. She would quickly call the Guardians and turn him over to them.

But it was equally obvious that she had no idea who he was. Her magic shield worked against the Guardians as well as against demons like him, so she had unwittingly kept herself isolated from those who could have warned her about the danger of his presence. She thought he was a Shifter. Perhaps she thought humans had hurt him. He almost laughed at the thought. What would she say if she knew it was those on the side of the angels who were hunting him? She was helping the wrong guy and she had no idea.

It was amusing really. He should take advantage of her ignorance

He settled back on the soft pillows. "You can look at the leg. Not that I need you to. I can heal myself on my own."

"I can tell you have strong magic," she said gravely. "I don't know what kind of arcane you are."

She left it open, not quite a question, but a comment that would allow him to fill her in if he chose to. He said nothing. It was better she filled in the blanks with her own mistaken assumptions. That way he could claim in the future that he had not lied to her.

She pulled back the blankets to examine his leg. She brought a pitcher of water and gently sponged the tooth marks and puncture wounds around his ankle.

"The sharp prongs of the trap pierced your calf right through to the bone," she remarked. "But you do have incredible healing powers. Your bone is knitting back together already. The soreness and pain you feel now is your body healing."

"I know that," he said.

She flashed a smile at him, not offended by his remark. The water felt soothing beyond simple coolness of the damp sponge. Now he was certain she was using some magic on him, her healing magic. He could see the glow of light, some strange mixture of Elemental Water and Elemental Stone that kneaded his flesh and blood back into its healthy state.

When she finished, he was amazed to see that there was no sign whatsoever that he had ever been injured. Even his own healing took much longer than that.

"That's amazing," he blurted.

"I know that." She tossed him a saucy smile.

Touché.

～

After she healed his leg, Naya fed him some broth, infused with more herbs and minerals that would help his body regain its strength. She was also aware of how starved he had been recently, and that only his incredible stamina had limited the extent of the damage that had been done. He would need more food than her broth of pine nuts and mushrooms would provide. Very likely he was a carnivore. He had that look to him. She did not eat meat herself; in fact, she didn't even usually eat grains, only veggies, fruit, nuts, and mushrooms. If he stayed longer, she would have to get meat. She didn't object to others eating meat, aware that for certain animals it was as natural as any other part of the circle of life. She didn't really enjoy the smell in her kitchen, however.

It probably won't be a problem, she reminded herself. He had made it clear that he considered every moment he spent with her to be an imposition. He was obviously one of those guys who didn't trust anyone and didn't want to be in anyone's debt. He would leave as quickly as he had showed up in her life and she would likely never see him again. She was used to that. Most of the patients she found in the woods were strangers, some human, some arcane, and she healed them without ever finding out the stories behind the journey that brought them into her life briefly.

She felt like a tree next to a river. Things floated by her and while they were near, she provided them with shade and sometimes with sustenance if they needed it. Then, inevitably, they floated on down the current while she remained rooted in the place she was; not completely unchanging, but growing slowly in comparison to the rest of the world around her.

The Dryad part of her was absolutely contented with this lifestyle. In fact, the Dryad in her envied her Hamadryad, Quigley, who truly was rooted in place and never moved. There were days when Naya wished she could live like that. Days when her business in the human world were just too hectic and too overwhelming, Naya wished she could lie down next to the river and simply drink peace from the loam.

But there were other days when the other half of her, the part she tended to think of as the human side of her, but perhaps it was better to think of it as the Water side of her, felt restless and impatient. She felt like she needed to *go some-where* and *do something*. She wanted to travel and see the world. She wanted... more. Something more.

People needed her here, she reminded herself. If she needed something more out of life, the river would bring it to her. She didn't need to travel anywhere to find fulfillment. She didn't need to be more than she was right now. She had never been ambitious, and she wasn't about to start setting her sights on advancement for its own sake. That just wasn't her style.

And yet she felt empty when she thought about how the man in her spare room would leave and go on and probably do exciting things and she would never even know what those were or where he was or what he was doing without her.

What a strange line of thought this is. She shook herself. Wake up, girl, she chastised herself. You have work to do.

When had she last checked in with her tree? Oh no! Quigley had asked her to get water from the special pool and Naya had been so distracted when she found the man by the river, that she had never gone all the way to the waterfall with the pool of the correct water. In fact, she had even thought when she came across him that perhaps that was the reason she had been sent in that direction, but she had totally forgotten about the fact that her tree had specifically requested that she bring the water from the pool back and water his roots with it.

It would take too long for her to walk back up that way. She would have to take her pick-up truck. That reminded her of the man's pick-up truck in the gravel driveway next to her house. He had seemed concerned about it. Like most guys, he was probably attached to his truck. She couldn't blame him, since it had obviously been souped up and was a pretty sweet ride. She reckoned it could carry a load of tree trunks with no problem. It was so customized she couldn't tell what make it had been originally, although she wasn't that big of an expert on machines. Maybe she would ask one of the crews later, if she had a chance. Then she worried that maybe he wouldn't like her showing off his truck to other guys. Some men were more possessive of their trucks than of their girlfriends. She giggled at the thought.

Her patient fell asleep, so she left him a note, reminding him that he was welcome to stay as long as he wanted, there was more broth in the fridge, but if he wanted to leave, she would understand. She left his keys on the note.

❧

August 6, Saturday, Late Afternoon
Waxing Gibbous Moon

By the time that Vass woke up again, he could see from the hue and slant of the sunlight coming through the window that it was late afternoon. It was summer so the days were long, but in the mountains the sun set earlier than in the main town, lower in the valley.

He felt completely healed. The woman had only given him a weird nutty broth to drink and yet he felt more satiated than he had after stuffing himself with a huge feast back home. Of course, that food had other advantages. If he had eaten the food of Darkpyre, he would have his magic back by now. He needed to get his powers back.

Other than that, though, he felt better than he had in a long time. Better than he had in years in fact.

Instinctively, he wondered how he wanted to dispose of the woman. Enslave her? Even in hell, healers were useful. She would not work willingly, but it would be easy to make her serve the Demon King by threatening other people. He knew her type and her type's weakness. Torture her directly and she would resist the physical pain until she was so physically broken she would be no use to the demons by the time she agreed to serve them. Torture a little kid in front of her and she would do anything to make it stop. So predictable.

He wondered if her brand of Elemental magic would really be worth the trouble of enslaving her. Sure, it felt great right now, but he had been experiencing a bad stretch. Was it really preferable to the healing that a Harpy could provide by vomiting in your mouth? That might not feel as warm and fuzzy, but it did the job. Besides, did his father really need any more healers? Probably not.

If Vass didn't capture her and enslave her, he should probably kill her. Again, that would be trivial to do now that he was feeling better. He didn't even need magic to do it. She was so unguarded around him, that even though she currently had more magic than he did, he knew he could just slip up behind her and slit her throat and she would never see it coming. It was always better to tidy up any encounters with any magical creature that had seen you weak and vulnerable. She had seen him weak and vulnerable. He ought to kill her.

For some reason, though, he didn't want to do that. Why not? He couldn't think of anything. All he could think about was her beautiful dual-colored eyes, her smile, the saucy way she had thrown his own words back at him and the gentle feel of her hands on his skin...

His arousal in her presence... Of course. He was such an idiot. He didn't want to kill her because she was a sexy wench. He should bang her. When she came back, he would turn on the charm, or maybe just grab her and just pin her under him on the same bed he had been laying in this whole time and screw her brains out. He would make her scream in pain until she started screaming in pleasure. He could make her writhe under him, begging for climax. He was certain he had enough magic to make her desire him.

Weird, but he didn't want to do that either.

He felt restless and stood up. She washed his clothes. He couldn't believe her audacity. His clothes were torn up rags, why would she think he would want those back? Why hadn't she bought him new clothes? Then he saw that she had carefully sewn all of the tears. Where too much material had gone missing, she had patched it with material that was obviously as close as she could find. It still made him look like Raggedy Andy, an old kids' toy he remembered tearing apart one time while throwing a temper tantrum. Was that a childhood memory? Where did that come from? Mostly he blocked out his childhood memories. When he allowed to himself to remember, he remembered himself being a spoiled brat. Fancy parties, pony rides. Presents and cakes, servants praising him for an effort he never made.

There were other parts of his childhood too, beatings, being locked in dark, tight spaces, mockery from his father. Things he didn't care to dwell on. Even as a prince, he had been weak as a child, and among his kind, the weak were taunted and punished for their weakness. That was for the best. A child had to learn to trust no one to grow strong. If he hadn't grown strong, he would have died. That was the way of the world.

He searched through the cottage. If he wasn't going to enslave her, kill her, or rape her, then at least he could take whatever he needed from her house for his own use. But she had nothing worth stealing. Finally, he took the keys that she had left to him and went outside and looked at the truck he had stolen from the man he had pushed over a cliff. With any luck, his former friend had died...

That was extremely unlikely. Chet was a Guardian now and he was just as strong, if not stronger than, Vass. He was probably alive, back at the Magician's Castle or wherever he hung out these days, planning his revenge. He was probably pissed as hell that Vass had tricked him, thrown him off a cliff, and stolen his truck.

Didn't seem like a good idea to take the truck. Vass decided to leave it with the woman. Maybe he could leave her as a future resource, he decided. Instead of burning any bridges now, why not let her think he felt gratitude for what she had done for him?

He wrote her a note. He tried to make it sound "sweet." Vass wasn't very good at sweet, but he thought it looked pretty good.

Thanks, beautiful. You saved my life. Take the truck as payment. I don't want to be in your debt. Ha ha.

He didn't know her name and he didn't tell her his. He had written the words 'ha ha' to show that he was just joking about not wanting to be in her debt, even though it was absolutely true. He wasn't sure if that was a normal thing for humans or just big among demons, so he tried to make it look like a joke just to be on the safe side. Sure, she thought he was a Shifter, not a demon, but Shifters were a lot more like humans than demons were.

So instead of doing anything bad to her or taking anything from her, he was leaving her a gift. It felt a little weird. His father would kill him if he ever found out. No, worse. His father would laugh at him. His father would despise him.

What else is new? he thought cynically. His father already thought Vass was a complete joke and held him in utter contempt. Vass was going to have to do some terrible things to win back the Demon King's respect.

But he didn't have to start here. He didn't have to start with *her*, the Dryad who had saved him. She really had saved his life, he thought, suddenly shocked by the realization. He had written that in the note thinking he was exaggerating, but now that he thought about it, he realized the poison in the trap would have eventually killed him.

And it was his former friend who had done that to him, Vass fumed, it was Chet who trapped him in such a way that even if he wasn't able to bring him in to the Guardians, eventually he would die.

You f'king bastard, thought Vass. As soon as I have my power back, I will get my revenge. I'll make you experience all the pain and humiliation that you made me go through! I will take away your magic, then your friends, including your lovely little elf wife, and then I will torture you until you beg for death. And then I will make sure you are reincarnated in Darkpyre as a slave.

Satisfied with his dark thoughts, that were more like his usual self, he left the house of the Dryad and hiked back into town. He had work to do if he was going to regain his former glory as a prince of hell...

Four

August 6, Saturday, Sunset
Waxing Gibbous Moon

NAYA DROVE her truck as far to the falls as she could. She couldn't make it all the way to the head of the falling water, but the road did allow her to make it close to the pool that collected it at the base of the waterfall.

She took her pitcher out and clambered over rocks, roots, and brush to kneel by the side of the water. As she bent down to gather water in the pool, she sensed a huge force of Elemental magic gathering around her. A face shimmered in the water behind her own reflection in the pool. Gasping, she looked up at the waterfall.

The face appeared to be created by the mist and splashing water. It was nothing permanent. The features shifted subtly with the mist, ever-changing, vaguely female, vaguely ancient, gentled by the wrinkles of wisdom. The white foam seemed to swirl like hair around the wise and magnificent visage. The face contoured by the waterfall was as large as that of a giantess.

Or a goddess.

Naya knew she was seeing the face of the river goddess, Miqwe, a Water Elemental as old and powerful as the river that ran through Arcana Glen itself. There were no river goddesses on Earth, except those, like this one here, who had come from other Spheres. Water Elementals such as this spirit, came from the magical realm Springvale. Sometimes the river appeared as a matron, completely crystal and transparent. But right now, she appeared as a giant woman who starred directly down at Naya.

"NAYA FAIRCHILD." The deep yet feminine voice that emerged from the waterfall thundered as loudly as the falls themselves. Naya heard the voice as much in her heart as she did with her ears. Nonetheless the words were clear to her.

"WHY HAVE YOU NOT YET ANSWERED THE CALL?" asked the river goddess.

Naya tilted her head. "I was not sure what I had heard..."

"YOU WERE CALLED IN WINTER, WHEN MY WATERS SLUMBERED UNDER ICE. YET THE CALL AWAKENED ME AND IT SHOULD HAVE AWAKENED YOU."

Naya remembered having the clear sensation of an important change washing over her in January of this year. Every month since, the feeling of needing to do something had grown stronger. And yet, in the end, a feeling was just a feeling. She didn't know how to respond to it.

"YET YOU DID NOT ANSWER," chided the river goddess.

"I don't feel worthy, goddess of the river," Naya said said honestly. "I couldn't believe the call was meant for me."

"SEVEN PULSES OF THE MOON HAVE PASSED," observed the goddess. "BEFORE THE MOON PULSES AGAIN, YOU MUST ANSWER THE CALL."

Naya trembled. "But how...?"

"YOU KNOW HOW."

"But I don't!" Naya cried stubbornly. "I can feel my power is stronger, but what am I to do with my skills that I'm not already doing?"

The cliff of boulders on the slope next to the waterfall shifted subtly; the shape they made, always vaguely anthropomorphic, now shuddered into prominence, clearly the form of a giant stone man, an elder with a long beard of moss and lichen. Stone blinked and opened, revealing deep, sentient eyes that stared down at Naya. He was an Elemental Stone spirit, a mountain god, from another mystical Sphere, Autumndelle. Here on Earth, he had married the river goddess. He was her husband, and had been, from time immemorial, since they had first arrived here, met and mated.

His voice was even deeper than the river's. It wasn't a sound so much as it was an earthquake that rattled Naya's entire body.

"TELL THEM WHO YOU ARE," rumbled the mountain god. "YOU ARE THE ONE WHO CAN UNITE THE WATERS OF SPRING AND AUTUMN, OF SUMMER AND WINTER, OF PAST AND FUTURE. YOU ARE THE ONE WHO BRINGS BALANCE AND HARMONY."

"But why me...?" What have I done to deserve this? she wondered.

"TELL THEM WHO YOU ARE."

"But how do I...?" began Naya.

"CLAIM YOUR POWER."

"But who would believe...?" begged Naya.

The mountain god shut his rocky eyelids again, and the impression of his body settled back into a chaotic formation of rock. It was hard for Elementals to awaken in the Mundane Sphere for any length of time, and the Stone Elementals were the hardest of all to rouse.

"HOW MUCH CLEARER DO YOU NEED THE CALL TO BE, CHILD OF THE STREAM AND EARTH?" demanded the river goddess. She sounded at once amused, annoyed and compassionate. "YOU ARE THE GUARDIAN

OF TEMPERANCE. GO TO THE TEMPLE AND ASCEND YOUR THRONE."

"I will do as you say," promised Naya. Her whole body trembled. *But what if they don't believe me?*

An image blossomed in her mind. She saw herself make a new urn and gather the water from the pool beneath the waterfall of the river goddess and the mountain god.

Pour the waters out before them and they will recognize you. The final voice that bespoke her was deepest of all, neither male nor female, from no recognizable source. It glowed with power, as if it grew from the Light of creation itself; and yet it welled up, not from outside, but from deep inside her, from the core of her spirit. In that instant, she saw her doubts for what they were: fear. And as soon as she perceived her fear for what it was, it vanished.

The river goddess sank back to sleep as the mountain god had, yet for a wondrous moment, the entire glade remained luminous, permeated with wonder and mystery, alive with a light that was brighter than sunlight. No doubt, no fear, no conflict existed, no division at all between self and universe. The boundary dissolved and Naya breathed in quiet glory.

The moment of utter clarity passed, but the patina of bliss remained, like the taste of sweetness on the tongue after a bit of fruit was consumed.

How much clearer could the Call be? The river goddess was right. For months now, Naya had heard the Call but doubted it. Indecision had torn her in two. This was the true source of the restlessness she had been feeling, the water in her nature urging her to do more, to make something new grow and to bring change into the world.

And yet the stone part of her nature had held her back. Obligations weighed her down. And not just her sense of obligation to the community, although that was huge. How would her business fare if she left it behind? What would her employees do if she quit her job to become a Guardian? Who would take care of her tree or the trees of the other dryads if she were not here to protect them?

Beneath that was the nagging fear that she wasn't worthy. Who was she to demand to be appointed a Guardian—one of the Twenty-two most powerful magic users in the Seven Mortal Spheres? She wasn't a Seraph or a Dragon, a Hero or a Wizard. She was only a simple Dryad. She was a modest healer who ran a timber mill. Just an ordinary person, a nobody in the grand scheme of things.

She had so many questions. She had so many duties already tugging at her. She didn't want to leave where she was or the people who relied on her. It would be a betrayal. Naya wasn't ambitious but this was an ambitious goal. She wasn't proud but this was a goal that demanded she take pride in her abilities and bruit them before the world.

But if she didn't accept the Calling, she would be like a dam bursting at the seams, bringing destruction rather than new life. She must have been given this new surge of power for a reason. It wasn't that she was doing things differently than she had ever done before. She had the same talents, but there was a new strength to them. Take her healing of the Shifter's leg. In the past, she would have only been able to hurry the healing along, not completely erase the scars as if they had never even been there. Her healing had leaped to a whole new level.

That should have confirmed everything she thought she knew about the Calling. But it only made her more afraid and uncertain. Her doubts circled around and around the same issues, like a whirlpool. What was so great about her that she deserved a new torrent of power? And suppose she did have stronger abilities, wasn't it wrong to turn her back on her community now that she had more power? She only had as much skill as she did, after all, because of what other people had shared with her whole life. To simply abandon them once she was strong, rather than give back to the community that had nurtured her, just felt wrong.

And yet how could she ignore the injunction of the Elementals and the Light itself?

With all these questions still swirling around in her mind, she brought the water of Miqwe Falls to her tree. The Hamadryad absorbed the special water gladly. His bark face formed a picture of contentment.

"That hits the spot." He opened one eye and winked at her knowingly. "And I take it you had a conversation with someone?"

"You might have told me that the Elementals wanted to speak to me," Naya rebuked him.

"The river goddess has been shouting at you for months now," he countered calmly. "You were ignoring her."

"Not *ignoring* her."

"Oh? There's another word for pretending you don't hear someone who is shouting your name?"

"I've been busy," she said defensively. "Anyway, you got your wish. She told me what she wanted to say. She wants me to be the new Guardian of Temperance."

"Perfect for that, aren't you," remarked Quigley.

"But what about you and the other trees? Who will protect you?"

"There are other Dryads who could do the job. Even a Faun, like your friend Sylvia, could do the job. Although she's a bit too rambunctious for my taste. Always running from one place to another like a wild goat." The tree made a face that made Naya laugh.

"Sylvia is fantastic, but she doesn't have a sense of responsibility."

"And *you* have an overburdened sense of responsibility. Other people can do things to help you. It doesn't *always* have to be about you helping others. Being in a community means accepting that you are not the only tree who holds up the whole forest."

"Is that what I've been doing?" Naya cried, aghast. "Have I been arrogant?"

"Oh, sure," said Quigley sarcastically. "That's definitely your big problem. Arrogance." He snorted, then sobered. "Arrogance is not your weakness, heartwood. I would describe it more as indecision. At some point, you can't balance everything. You have to make a choice. You can't stay still any longer. You have to move forward. And it is acceptable to want more out of life, Naya. It is well to recognize that you deserve more sometimes when you have worked hard to earn it."

~

August 7, Sunday
Waxing Gibbous Moon

Vass owned a house in Arcana Glen. It was one of the mansions of the hillside community, where the rich humans who came to ski had their "winter cottages": meaning a house with fifty rooms and a chandelier. That was exactly the kind of house that many arcanes also kept for themselves, including Vass. Before he had fallen on hard times and lost his magic, thanks to his former friend turned nemesis, he had enjoyed a human cover life as a rich playboy. He had traveled all around the Earth, owned a villa in Italy, a chalet in Switzerland, a yacht in the Mediterranean, a smaller yacht the local lake, and an island in the Caribbean.

Technically, he still owned all of that under his human identity. His father had such contempt for Earth that he hadn't bothered to take it away in the same manner he had stripped his son of all his mansions and estates in Darkpyre.

When Vass had checked the mundane bank, after he'd recovered from being a pig but before Chet attacked, they showed him his account, including his vault. His secret stash of gold and bills and passports and useful magical items—tools that he could use even in his current dilapidated state—were still there.

His mansion was still on the hill. Since Vass traveled so much, not only to other worlds but around this one, he had a caretaker/butler/bodyguard to attend him when he was in Arcana Glen and to keep the mansion in good condition during his absence. The man was a human, an ugly thug, thoroughly mundane, but aware that arcanes existed because plenty of arcanes had tried to kill him.

"What's your name?" Vass asked. The guy had worked for Vass for fifteen years, but all humans kind of blended together for Vass. Vass snapped his fingers. "No, don't tell me. I remember. Yuri."

"Da, boss," The big, tatted thug was very old school.

"Prague, right? That's where we met. But you're from..."

"Belarus."

"Human." Vass yawned.

"Da, boss."

Yuri knew Vass was a demon. Yuri came from a mafia involved in some dark cult stuff that included summoning demons and other stupid shit. This cult had "summoned" and "commanded" some Guliks—Glutton Demons—that belonged to Vass's dad, the Gulik Demon King Xin Glu'ulgros. Xin sent his son to clarify the pecking order for the dumbf*cks. Vass arrived and casually mutilated and murdered every one of the mafia thugs who rushed to attack him, which was about two-thirds of them. Finally, the chickenshit leader of the thugs ordered Yuri, then about seventeen, to stay behind and fight, while he and the rest of this gang retreated.

Yuri, terrified out of his wits, had nonetheless advanced to fight Vass. Vass had decided the kid showed some promise. Not so stupid as to rush into a fight, but brave and loyal enough to fight if he had no choice. Vass used Dark magic to casually smack the kid around the room—without even touching him—just to show he could—and then asked if Yuri wanted to live and serve him.

Yuri had seemed pretty enthusiastic about the opportunity.

Vass could have made Yuri formally sign over his soul but had never bothered. Vass had already spared Yuri's life, which would have been payment enough for his labor, but Vass thought it would look better if he gave his "butler" a salary, so he did. Yuri had apparently used the money to pay for a younger sister to go to boarding school somewhere. For obvious reasons, Yuri didn't want to introduce Vass to his younger sister, and Vass didn't press. There was no point upsetting his butler, and for some reason, humans tended to get bent if you banged their sisters.

Yuri didn't comment on Vass's raggedy appearance but fetched Vass the accouterments for a bath.

"Do you vant I fetch you voman?" Yuri asked.

Vass thought of Naya. It would be delightful to share a bath with her... But Yuri meant a professional, either a mundane hooker or a succubus. Surprising himself, Vass declined. But he did accept a long soak in the sauna and a brand-new designer silk suit.

After he was feeling more like himself again, he contemplated going skiing. Then he remembered it was August. He didn't have his big yacht here; that was still moored at a blue and white city somewhere in Greece, but he did have a smaller yacht on Mystic Lake.

Then he remembered that he had sent Raziel to live on the yacht.

"Zerre vas call for you, boss," said Yuri. "Construction vorrker called you to talk about Big Project. He said it vas very urgent, big problem."

Vass grunted. Construction worker? What the hell.

"Fallen angel also call," said Yuri. "He said he had to talk to you about Big Project too. Vas very urgent, zerre vas big problem."

"The same big problem?" asked Vass.

Yuri spread his hands as if he were totally ignorant. "Vat do I know, boss?"

Vass snorted. But Yuri could play dumb all day and twice as long on Tuesday.

"Call them both back and tell them to meet me at the yacht," said Vass.

Five

August 7, Sunday
Waxing Gibbous Moon

INTELLECTUALLY, Naya could understand what her tree friend was trying to tell her. But recognizing that she tortured herself with indecision didn't make her debate less agonizing about what to do next. Thoughts cascaded through her mind as she drove her truck back to the watermill.

The Elemental Spirit had told her: GO TO THE TEMPLE AND ASCEND YOUR THRONE. The Temple must mean the *N'hara Sarmateem* – the Temple of the Guardians. Legend claimed the Temple was a mystical basilica that simultaneously existed in all worlds, and in none, with twenty-two thrones about a round table. It was the meeting place of the *Melkara Sarmateem*, the Council of Guardians. The Guardians guarded the Gates between the Seven Mortal Spheres and Three Immortal Spheres, the ten distinct worlds that grew like fruits upon the Cosmic Tree, the Tree of Worlds, the *Akulat Kh'adnateem*.

The words of the ancient tongue poured through her memory. She had learned all this as a young Dryad, when she'd still lived in her clan's grove in Autumndelle. Just thinking about it now daunted her. She knew she had to answer the Calling...

But... but...

One didn't simply walk into the Temple of the Guardians. Access could only be granted, in pragmatic terms, by the Magician and the Fool, the two Guardians who headed the Council. They lived in Arcana Castle here in Arcana Glen. Reaching them wasn't easy, however. They might be close to Naya geographically, but they were worlds apart from her socially.

Besides, even if they welcomed her, there were still many things she had to do here first to prepare for such a huge move. The river goddess had given Naya a timeline: before they next pulse of the moon. To a Water Elemental, the "pulse" of the moon meant one Full Moon and one New Moon. The Full Moon this August fell on August 16; the New Moon, on August 27. She had to go to the Castle by the end of the month. Fine. She would try to wrap up everything here with her timber business in that amount of time.

Then Naya remembered that she also had to make a new ewer. The vision implanted in her by the Light made that clear. She'd made plenty of vessels before, so she wasn't worried about if she could do, only if she could do it *well*. It would mean sourcing the right clay, throwing the pot, painting it, glazing it, and firing it. Already she could see a design in her mind eye, a mixture of blue and earth tones, with flecks of gold and silver to represent the light of the sun and the moon.

~

August 7, Sunday
Waxing Gibbous Moon

"You look like hell, Raz," said Vass. "And you stink like a cesspool. Get up! Tell me what was so urgent."

Raziel Renaci blinked blearily at Vass. Raziel Renaci, once a respected judge in the human world and a respected angel in the arcane world, was officially fallen: he had renounced the Light and sold his soul to Vass's father, Xin Glug'ulgros. Now Raziel had no choice but to serve his demon masters. In January of this year, Xin had entrusted Vass with the black feather that constituted Raziel's official "leash," the tangible totem Raziel had surrendered when he sold his soul. The feather wasn't a literal feather; rather, it was a wisp of light from Raziel's wings. Now it acted like a chain, binding Raziel to the will of whoever held it. Vass didn't have to manifest the feather physically to control Raziel, though, in the early days, when Raziel had still been quite stubborn, Vass had sometimes pulled the feather out of the ether to physically force the angel to comply with his commands.

The Fallen Angel did look terrible. His once sleek and beautiful black wings were tattered, filthy, mutilated, and missing feathers. One wing was twisted in a funny position as if it might be broken. There were circles under Raziel's eyes, and his once strong physique looked gaunt. His flesh sported a map of scars, silvery lacerations and lesions of necrotic flesh, and he held his arm at a funny angle as if it had been broken and reset wrong.

The stench came from the dead flesh.

Vass had a sudden flashback of memory. He remembered when he was an animal and everyone else around him was laughing at him, kicking him, and worse. Vass's own half-brothers had been eager to see Vass torn apart alive by the hounds. Only one man had defended him: Raziel.

Because Raziel had tried to defend Vass (even after he had been turned into a pig), Vass's father had decided to make an example of the angel. Raziel had been accused of being a traitor by Vass's father and tortured in front of the Demon Kings. The places where Raziel's flesh had refused to heal, the stinking puss-filled welts, were places where Xin had literally bitten him, with his venomous, razor-sharp teeth. Not even an angel could heal the venomous bite of a demon.

Vass wasn't clear how they had escaped that, but he knew that Raziel had picked him up and carried him out of there. He wanted to say something like, 'hey, thanks.' Something like, 'if it weren't for you, I would still be in that place in the form of a helpless, humiliated animal.' Something like, 'you were the only one who proved to be a real friend.' Something like, 'You have been a better brother to me than any of my own kin ever have.'

But that was cringe as f*ck. Vass would never say something like that. It was almost more humiliating than being a swine.

So instead, Vass tried to say something helpful. "You're filthy and disgusting, Raz, and your body isn't healing itself properly."

Raziel grimaced. "I know, Vass."

The Fallen Angel looked up. His body seemed cloaked in shadow, like an inverse halo. By the time that Vass had first met Raziel, the angel had already fallen. Raziel had black wings surrounded by dark fire. Supposedly, he had made his wings look snowy white to other angels, although Raziel claimed his wings had always been black, but that, yes, he'd once had a halo, a nimbus of light around him, shining like radiant silver and gold rather crackling like a dark storm. Vass personally thought the dark storm looked cooler.

Yet even that terrible power had faded into a shade of its former strength. The first time Vass met Raziel, the Fallen Angel's wings were powerful, blazing with dark fire and the man himself had been a complete badass in battle. He had been tested in the arena against Wrath Demons the first time he was taken to Darkpyre, and Raz had busted seven in a row.

Now Raziel looked like he couldn't even fight off a pixie on a bad hair day.

"We are being hunted by both sides now," said Raziel. "It's only a matter of time before one or the other catches us. How did you escape the Guardian? It was Chet, wasn't it?"

"Funny story," said Vass. "A pretty girl saved my life. And she turned out to also be a really good healer. She might even be able to fix your smell. She's a Dryad. She…"

"By the Light," said Raziel, "You don't mean Naya the Dryad do you?"

"Do you know her? Did you used to shag her maybe?"

"Don't be an ass. Of course, I know her. I lived in Arcana Glen for years before I openly went to your side, remember? I know her and she would recognize me as Judge Renaci."

"Yeah, but I think she still wouldn't kill you. She's stupid like that."

"I would never go to her."

"But I told you…"

"Yes," said Raziel impatiently. "I know she would heal me even though she disapproves of what I've done. That's exactly why I wouldn't… Look, it's a sin you can appreciate. It's called pride. I can never go to any of my former friends and ask for help. I don't deserve it anymore."

"Okay, okay, don't bite my head off. We're only waiting for one other person to arrive and then we can… Oh, there, I see him."

The yacht was still at the dock. A man still wearing a hard hat and dirty dungarees looked out of place in the rich man's marina.

John Helwall, the "construction worker" who had called Vass, was the grandson of the man who owned the construction company working on the Big Project. He was also an Ice Giant. Even in his human form, he was immense, like a circus Strong Man or pro-wrestler. Raziel and Vass had both worked with him before, which was fortunate. No one had bothered to tell John that Vass was in disgrace.

The three men shook hands and chewed through some small talk.

"So what's the problem, John?" Vass asked. "Your company can't handle building the project specifications?"

"We can handle the structure just fine," said John sourly. "We built on the spot that your lot demanded, on the pinnacle of a mountain, crazy as that was. But what are you going to do about energy? There's no leylines of magic in the spot where you had us build. It's like building a skyscraper with no electricity or plumbing." John continued, growing ever more dyspeptic, "Supposedly it was going to be powered by the detonation of a 'super weapon like a magical nuclear bomb,' but first of all, you don't power a building with a bomb, you power it with a power plant. I don't care if the energy source is nuclear, solar or cow farts. Second, that promised power source was apparently stolen when a specimen from the laboratory at the base escaped with it. So that plan is a non-starter."

"Does anyone else know about this problem?" asked Vass eagerly.

"No."

"Fantastic!" Vass rubbed his hands together.

John glowered at him. "If you're thinking of killing me and sweeping this under the rug, think again, demon. You can't just make this problem go away by ignoring it."

"No, no, I'm going to solve your problem," said Vass. "Uh... there *is* a solution isn't there? You're a builder-guy. What would you suggest?"

"Buy the land adjacent to the mountain where we're currently building. That land is rich in leylines. We tap the magic, and bam. We have electricity and plumbing, or better yet, the magical equivalent."

"John," declared Vass, clapping his hands on the man's shoulders, "I promise I will get this for you."

"Don't touch me," said John flatly.

Vass pulled back his hands, smirking.

"Get us the land and your Tower will light up like a Christmas Tree," promised John.

After he left, Raziel said, "You were quick to promise him that land. It might not be that easy to acquire real estate in Arcana Glen. There are arcane families and clans who have lived on the land for decades, some for centuries. And no one's going to sell to a demon."

"Raziel, don't you see? This is the answer to everything. This is how we get back in good with my father!"

~

Vass and Raziel discussed how they would pitch the plan. Vass would do most of the talking, since in theory, Raziel was his slave, broken and cowed. The angel certainly looked broken; only Vass knew that was not true. Although one thing was clear. Raziel wasn't looking forward to a trip back to Darkpyre.

"There's an alternative you know," Raziel said. "To returning to Darkpyre."

"I don't see what," said Vass. "As you pointed out, we're currently being hunted by both sides. We can't hide forever."

"You could defect to the Guardians," said Raziel softly. "You could tell them about the plans of the Dark Triad. Warn them about the Project. And the Super Weapon. John thinks the Super Weapon is lost, but personally, I wouldn't count on that. You know what would happen if it's used."

"You want me to betray my father?" Vass asked.

Raziel passed his hand over his face. "I don't know, Vass. The man found out you had been transformed into a swine by an angry paramour, and instead of transforming you back, as he easily could have, his response was sentence you to be ripped apart by starving Hell Hounds while everyone you know watched and laughed. Not to mention his intentions for the rest of the cosmos. Does he deserve your loyalty?"

"Shut up!" shouted Vass. "You are not allowed to insult my father! You're no better than the rest of us, Raziel! You're worse because you're a traitor! And now you want me to turn my back on my people like you turned your back on yours? To be a traitor, like you? You're scum! Guess what? I'm not! I am a Prince of Darkpyre and I *want* demons to rule the Tree of Worlds! That's how it should be!"

Raziel hunched his shoulders. Vass paced and planned their itinerary over and again, with small variations, trying to work out the perfect approach to impress his father, but Raziel only sat quietly, staring at the wall. He didn't speak again.

Finally, when Vass felt ready, he made the call he had long anticipated and also dreaded. He called his father.

Six

August 8, Monday

MAKING HER MONDAY ROUNDS, Naya stopped at the Tree & Shrub Nursery run by her best friend, Posey Pollenpuff, a Flower Fairy, or Anthousai, from Springvale. Naya ordered all the new trees that she wanted to plant in the forest from Posey's Tree & Shrub Nursery.

Naya trotted through the nursery filled with little growing seedlings. She was pleased to see that Posey was already talking to Sylvia Woodland. Sylvia was Naya's other best friend, a Faun whose family came from Autunmdelle. Yes, Naya knew that "best" usually meant the top of the list, a single person. Naya couldn't help it if she had two best friends who were equally dear to her.

Sylvia worked for Naya. The Faun was the chief Forestry Manager for Naya's timber company. In her other form, Sylvia had goat legs, goat horns and, ahem, bigger breasts. She was still quite buxom, even in her human form. She had thick chestnut hair, warm brown eyes with a glint of mischief, a vivacious smile and graceful, quick manner of movement that made it look as if she were always on the verge of skipping or leaping.

"...even other arcanes!" Sylvia was in the middle of a complaint to Posey. Sylvia paced back and forth between rows of container pots, while Posey bent over the pots, fussing over the sprouts in them.

"Even other arcanes do what?" asked Naya, as she entered the patio area with the rows of pots.

"Think that all Fauns are male!" declared Sylvia. "They don't understand that 'satyr' and 'nani,' are the proper terms for male and female Fauns. I was dating a guy who thought I was a demon! And you know what's worse?"

"Yes," teased Posey, "Because you've already told me several times, with increasingly colorful expletives."

"But I haven't told Naya yet!" declared Sylvia. She faced the Dryad. "Can you believe this guy, Naya? He dumped me because I *wasn't* a demon. I guess he had some fetish about dating a naughty demoness with goat horns and a forked tail, and when he found out that I wasn't a dominatrix from Darkpyre who would wear black spandex, whip him, and make him..."

"Please spare us the details," groaned Posey.

"—he said he needed 'space,' and then stopped returning my calls!" concluded Sylvia. "Where are all the good men? Who is hiding them?"

"Imagine how hard it is for the male nymphs," said Posey mischievously. "My brother complains about it all the time. He's an Anthousai, a flower fairy, and he complains that even if he gets any attention, it's all from other males. We have nothing against those who enjoy such, but he always develops hopeless crushes on curvy Shifter Bear women, who want nothing to do with him. He even proposed to Dezzie Boren—she told him that if he could defeat her in the fight ring, she'd grant him a date."

"The people who started all the problems are the humans," said Sylvia. "They see one of us and they think that represents our entire kind. They see a male faun and a female nymph and they think we only have one sex. How do they think we get babies?"

"Magic," laughed Posey.

Sylvia continued to itemize the problems with her last five or six male play-mates. Though Sylvia always complained that being a "Demi-human," (an archaic term for the arcanes from Autumndelle) made it impossible to find dates, especially a Faun, but Naya had never noticed Sylvia suffer any lack of male attention. She was casual about sex in way that Naya envied but could not imitate. Sylvia could genuinely enjoy a night with a guy, say goodbye the next morning, and have new fodder for her sarcastic critiques of the other sex. Naya always tried to hang on and fix whatever man she dated, and she always went for the most broken men around.

As if summoned out of her past, Riley Jefferson, the heartbreaker, appeared. He was also from Autumndelle. His problem was that he was a Werewolf—a Demi-shifter who became a humanoid shaped wolf covered with hair and with sharp fangs but still able to speak and walk like a man. The humans could not tell the difference between a werewolf, a Demi-human from Autumndelle, and a Wolf Shifter, a Lycan, a man who turned completely into a wolf. The later came from Winterdom, and usually served the Winter Elves. Finally, there was another kind of mystical creature that humans tend to call a Werewolf by mistake, a Hell Hound. A Hell Hound took the shape of a giant black dog with fiery red eyes who could turn into a man. Hell Hounds came from Darkpyre. They were technically a species of demon. Naya had tried to date a Hell Hound once too and vowed never to date a demon again. Talk about damaged...

Riley nodded his head at Naya. They were still friends even after their breakup. In fact, he still worked for her, the head of the crew of lumberjacks, or Forrest Clearance Operators, as they called them now.

"I have some news," Naya said to her to female best friends and her male best friend who had once been her lover. "I guess I should just tell you all at the same time since you're all here."

The three of them gathered around her. She breathed in the scent of the nursery, which was filled with flowers and seeds and growing things that she loved. What would it be like if she had to leave all this behind to go live in the town of Arcana Glenn, or worse yet, the scary looking Castle on the hill? The thought terrified her. Maybe what had been holding her up wasn't a sense of responsibility at all but just pure fear. She was just a coward when it came right down to it.

Angry at herself for her inability to move forward, she shook her head. She took a deep breath.

"Go on," said Sylvia. "Don't make us wait all day."

"Can't you see this is difficult for her?" asked Posey.

"Go on," urged Riley. "Just blurt it out, Naya. Even if it's bad news, whatever it is, you know we will help you through it."

They all echoed that, and their support only made her feel more terrible about announcing she was going to abandon them.

"For some time now I've been receiving a... kind of calling."

"A calling?" Sylvia wrinkled her brow. "Like on the phone?"

"I don't think she means on the phone," Riley said, rolling his eyes.

"Not on the phone, in my heart."

"Oh, that weird mumbo-jumbo stuff," scoffed Sylvia. Even though she was arcane herself, she had no patience for anything that she considered mystical. She didn't consider her own ability to shape shift to be mystical. It was just part of who she was. But if Naya discussed anything like *respecting the circle of life in the forest* or *heeding the mystical call of the great elemental gods and goddesses*, to Sylvia, that was as much nonsense as to any mundane human.

"Today the river herself spoke to me," Naya said. "The river spirit, Miqwe."

"Literally spoke," Sylvia echoed, her skepticism obvious.

"I saw her face in the waterfall and she literally spoke," said Naya. "She told me to accept the Calling. I am to apply to the Castle and try to become the new Guardian of Temperance."

Actually, the waterfall had been even more specific than that. The water goddess had not told Naya to "try to become" but she *was* the new Guardian of Temperance. But that sounded too arrogant to Naya, so she had rephrased it slightly. Still, it got the idea across, and her friends were suitably amazed.

Posey looked frightened. "But if you become the Guardian, aren't you going to have to leave? What will happen to Timber Falls?"

"I don't know," Naya admitted. "I may have to give it up. Maybe I can find a new owner."

Sylvia Woodland raised her hand. "Oh, me, me, me!"

Riley and Posey exchanged a glance of dismay. Without saying so, they conveyed the clear impression they did not think Sylvia was up to running Timber Falls. In fact, Naya was looking at Riley, thinking that if anyone could step into her shoes, it would be him.

He shook his head. "No way. I'm happy where I am."

"That's what I said too," said Naya. "I don't want to do this."

"Then don't," said Riley. "No one can force you to do anything you don't want to do, Naya. All they can do is ask. You can always refuse, even the call from the river goddess. It's up to you. You need to decide what you want to do. It's your future."

"Actually," Posey piped up, "It's all our future. If Naya goes, I think that means the end of Timber Falls. Sorry, Sylvia, but you know it's true. No one can replace Naya."

∼

Later that day, Naya had a visitor. The Timber Mill wasn't a tourist spot, and the whole forest was shielded, so it wasn't common to have random visitors. The shield only allowed in those in need. That included clients who needed good, ethically grown timber. It included stragglers who were injured and needed healing.

And today it included a Guardian.

Naya had been following the news about the Guardians being called two-by-two every month since January. It was an amazing thing to see. After the terrible Massacre of the Guardians, there had been no new Guardians called for a decade. And now so many were answering the call so fast, it seemed that the Council would be filled again.

The Magician, Guardian of the First Path and head of the Council, was the only Guardian from the old Council who had survived the massacre. For a long time, the Magician, Alephander Guiscard, had been the chief suspect in the murders for that very reason. However, in January, the Seraphs had tried and cleared Alephander Guiscard. The Seraphs also anointed a new Fool, Guardian of the Null Path. If the Magician was the head of the Council, the position of the Fool was equally important, as the Fool had veto power over any decision the Council made.

The Council was an archaic and strange institution. Like a tree, it grew from the deep-seated needs of sentient beings for order and harmony. And yet, it was far from a platonic ideal of utopian perfection. Maps of the Tree of Worlds always showed a symmetrical schematic of a hypothetical structure, perfectly formed and balanced, but the real cosmos was no more like that than a real tree was like a geometric diagram.

Just as a real tree grew according to its innate design, and yet always came out unique, oddly twisted and asymmetrical, bumpy and knobby, often leaning slightly to one side or the other, according to how it had grown up through years of drought and storms and sun and water, so it had been with the Council. The Council was *not* the government of the Tree of Worlds, although in the past, many ambitious Guardians had striven to make it so. The Council had grown up in response to the droughts and storms and occasional days of sunshine and cooperation in arcane history. Originally, the seed has been planted in the ash left by the firestorm of war. As with so many beautiful things, it would never have been planted had violence not first cleared the ground and made it necessary.

Back in some ancient age that even the Dryads could not clearly remember it, twenty-two rulers from the Seven Mortal Spheres had striven for supremacy over the entire *Akulat Kh'adnateem,* the Tree of Worlds. When they had almost destroyed the Tree itself, only then did they agree to sit together and make peace and strive to find a better way to guard the gates between the Spheres. They built the Temple of the Guardians permanently suspended in the ether between the worlds, with twenty-two thrones about a round table.

The strange names, titles, and usual recruitments of each of the Twenty-Two Guardians, the *Sarmarteem,* reflected this quirky history. The Magician and the Fool were almost always humans. The Emperor and Empress came from Summerland, and the citadel where they had their seat of power was in Summerland still. (Although now it was under control of the Winter Elves, who still occupied Springvale, Summerland and Autumndelle.) The High Priest, or the Hierophant, the Hermit and Death had traditionally been from Dayhaven. The Charioteer, the Hanged Man and the Devil—or the Pan—had been from Nightpyre. Fortune and Temperance had been from Springvale. The Sun and Judgment had been from Autumndelle. The Tower and the Moon had been from Winterdom. And so on for all of the Guardians.

Each title, each throne and crown of the round table had its own quixotic history, each title had exemplars who had been both glorious or horrific. No throne could claim to be all good or evil; each throne had, at some point in history, been seized by rogues who had abused their power. Guardians, like ordinary people, made choices according to the inner darkness or light in their own hearts. And that was why the *balance* of the Guardians was the true source of its power. It was the round table, and the fact that none, not even the most powerful among them, was allowed more sway than the others that kept the whole safe from the predations of any one of them.

And yet in every age, there were always those who saw that balance as nothing but an impediment to implementing their ideal world, their perfect platonic symmetry, their utopia. Never mind that they would have to kill the Tree of Worlds to "perfect" it. Such ambitious souls were always willing to sacrifice the real for the ideal, to destroy existence to make room for nothingness.

The ancient history of the Guardians was not taught in schools any longer, not even to arcane children. Naya reflected she was probably one of the few who had learned the old stories, the warning tales about how the Guardians could go wrong as well as they could do right. And so, although she respected the *Sarmateem* and their position, she was not one to grovel or play the sycophant when a guardian came to visit her.

"*Sarmati,*" she said, with an incline of her head that was the sketch of a bow but not a full bending of her body. "Please come talk in my office. You are Moxie Bridgestone, am I correct? The Guardian of Strength."

"Yes," Moxie Bridgestone said, "but today I am here on my own behalf, not on Guardian business. I hope you'll still see me."

"Of course," Naya said, intrigued by this humble plea.

Moxie was a petite woman, certainly not one that a casual observer would expect was one of the twenty-two most powerful magic users in the cosmos. She had fuzzy little cat ears sticking up on top of her head, in addition to her human ears. But the cat ears were not a costume. They were a real part of her body. Right now, they twitched nervously.

Traditionally, the Guardian of Strength was a lion shifter, but it wasn't clear if Moxie had that ability or if she was only a cat girl. It wouldn't change how Naya would treat her, and it wasn't her business, so Naya did not inquire. She invited Moxie to the porch of her cottage where comfortable handmade wooden chairs were positioned around a matching table. The cushions were hand-embroidered and stuffed with real goose down. Naya had made the cushions and a friend of hers had made the table and chair set.

"Thank you," said Moxie. She drew up her feet and sat in the lotus position on the bench, as if it were the most comfortable position in the world. She was very flexible.

Naya, by habit, sat up as straight as possible, and planted her feet firmly on the ground. "What can I do for you, *Sarmati*?"

"I'm looking for my brother," said Moxie. "I don't know if you're aware of my history, but I grew up as a prisoner, along with my brother, in a laboratory run by some very shady characters not far from here. Recently, I helped him escape. I was hoping he would join me, but he was afraid, I think, of the Guardians. He fled instead. I don't know what he had to do to escape, or if he may have been injured. I was wondering if maybe you had seen him. I know that many strays cross your land and that you help them. I don't know what name he would be using."

Instantly, the handsome stranger flashed through Naya's mind. She had suspected he might be a Shifter, although she wasn't able to detect what kind. Could he be a Lion Shifter? When she thought of his powerful, muscular body and the magical strength he had to recover so quickly from a poisonous trap, she knew it was definitely possible.

If Moxie was his sister, should she reveal the encounter?

"Does he know where you are?" Naya asked. "Does he know you're a Guardian?"

"I think so," she said. "He's... Sometimes it's hard to know what he's thinking. But I think he knows where to find me. I just don't know where to find him."

"Perhaps he does not wish to be found," said Naya. "If you want contact, I can certainly understand that, but if your brother doesn't, he must have his reasons."

"But if I could just find him..."

Naya shook her head. "I'm sorry. I can't tell you if I've seen him or not. I *can* tell you that even if I *had* seen him, I would not tell anyone about it, not even members of his own family, without his permission. It's not my place to share his secrets, or to share his location."

"You *do* know where he is!"

"I told you, I can't tell you if I know or don't know."

"If I make this Guardian business and I command you to tell me—"

"You have no authority to make me disclose such information," Naya reminded the Guardian gently. "Don't embarrass yourself by trying and making me refuse you officially."

Tears pricked Moxie's eyes. "Then I'm begging you. Please. It's very important and not just to me. I can't explain everything. But you have to know that if I can't find him, his life could be in danger!"

"His life is still his own to risk, and his secrets are still his own to keep," Naya said firmly. "I'm sorry. I can tell him, if I see him and know he is your brother, that you were looking for him, and that you believe it is very important."

A low growl started at the back of Moxie's throat. Naya suspected that the Shifter wasn't even aware of it. When Shifters were riled up, they tended to revert to animal behaviors. But Naya was no more worried than a tree would be disturbed by the growling of a lion. It would not change her mind or her position. On some issues, Naya was happy to go with the flow, to compromise, and to do whatever she could to make others happy. But on some issues, she planted her feet on the ground and would not be moved. This was one of those issues.

Finally, the growling stopped, and Moxie stood up. "Thank you for your help, although I wish you would have agreed to do more. But if you see him, tell him. Tell him I'm begging him to trust me and come to me. No one will hurt him. He doesn't have to be afraid of the Guardians."

"If you're a Guardian, your magic must be very strong," said Naya. "And I suspect your brother's magic is also very strong."

"Yes," Moxie said cautiously.

"Has it occurred to you that perhaps he is not hiding from you because he is afraid for himself? Perhaps he is hiding to keep *you* safe from *him*."

Moxie blinked. Understanding suffused her face. Thoughtfully, she stood up, thanked Naya for her time, and departed.

Seven

August 8, Monday
Waxing Gibbous Moon

THE LAST TIME Vass had been in Darkpyre, it had been hell for him. That might seem obvious, but usually for him, a visit to Darkpyre involved a posh pleasure den, intoxicating dishes and triturates, a series of orgies with other demons, further offers for pleasure from women willing to sell their bodies to him for a few crumbs, and servants and slaves and sycophants waiting on his every whim. Memories flooded Vass of walking these halls with Chet, back before the other demon had defected.

Chet was a low born mutt, Vas reminded himself. *It's no wonder he betrayed his people.*

Vass, on the other hand, had been born a prince. Every lesser demon kowtowed to him. Sycophants fawned over him, young females threw themselves at him, older males sought to do him "avuncular" favors because they saw such "promise" in him. A paparazzi of Harpies, Toadies and Leeches had crowded around him whenever he left his father's palace.

But when Vass lost his magic and then even his human form, the people he had thought were his friends—okay, he had never mistaken them for *friends*—but the people he assumed were respected colleagues—had turned on him instantaneously. He'd shown weakness, and that was never, ever allowed or forgiven.

That was why he had to return here to Darkpyre, even though it was the last place he wanted to go. It was also quite dangerous for him. He had no way of knowing if his father would accept his deal or if King Glug'ulgros would have Vass bound in chains, stripped, perhaps even transformed back into a swine.

Vass shuddered. He couldn't think of anything worse than that. He would rather be tortured even as a human being than be turned back into a pig to be

"

taunted and laughed at again. Fortunately, he didn't remember very much of his time he had spent in animal form. The curse that had been on him was different than that of a shape shifter. He had retained almost nothing of his human sentience. Therefore, just as an animal had a hard time remembering its own past, most of his memories from that time were of incoherent emotions, mostly fear.

This time would be different. Now, he was back in command of himself and soon he would be in command of the armies of hell again.

His king father was holding court in the Hall of the Seven Kings. Xin Glug'ul-gros liked to make the other Demon Kings wait on him, pretending to be his allies and friends, when everyone knew that he had conquered their territories and made them into his vassals. His father had once been considered the weakest of the seven demon kings, each of whom ruled through a specific vice. His father's vice was gluttony. However, gluttony was on the ascent these days. His father's powers had grown and now he ruled Hell.

As a son of the ruling King of Hell, that should've been enough for Vass to be feared and respected by the other demons. But Vass was not his father's only son. His father owned many slaves and impregnated many of them. He viewed his children as his property rather than his offspring. He would shower gifts upon those whom he favored, but he turned on them viciously without a moment's notice if he thought they failed him.

Vass made sure he showed no weakness as he swaggered into to the Hall of Seven Kings. The Hall had not changed since the dark ages, and still had the same feudal arrangement of a high table at the far end, lower rows of tables along the long walls of the rectangular room, and some kind of grisly torture for "entertainment" on a stage at the far end of the room. The Kings of the seven clans sat at the High Table, overseeing all the other demons. All the demons wore their demonic forms in the Hall.

No round tables for demons: the center throne sat above the other six. The High Throne showed which tribe was ascendent now. There were hundreds of kinds of demons and cursed souls who lived in Darkpyre, but seven clans had dominated for the last thousand years.

The Superbians, the Pride Demons, had lion heads, dragon wings, thorny horns, a peacock's tail and seven eyes. Superbians, who had often been the highest ranking tribe in centuries past, felt they should *still* be the true rulers of Darkpyre and were furious that one of their own didn't sit on the High Throne.

The Iragers, Wrath Demons, the soldiers of Darkpyre, had bull-heads and seething-hot volcanic skin. They liked to wear uniforms with lots of medals on their breasts, even in their demonic forms. They had wyvern wings and scorpion tails. Iregers, certain they should be the true rulers of Darkpyre, plotted constant coups and rebellions, furious that one of their own didn't sit on the High Throne.

The Acedians, Sloth Demons, had fuzzy moth wings with skull patterns, distended furry bodies like—well, like sloths—but (except in very young Acedians) instead of cute, sleepy snouts like the real animals, where their faces should have been, there was only a lump of sunken flesh crawling with maggots. Acedians felt they should be the true rulers of Darkpyre, although they were too lazy to fight for it, and were furious that one of their own didn't sit on the High Throne.

The Inviders, the Envy Demons, were tall and skeletal, with spindly chicken legs, tiny heads and long beaks like Ibis birds. They fancied themselves to be the greatest magicians of Darkpyre and most of them wore dark robes glittering with mystic symbols. They displayed gaudy jewelry fashioned from the skulls and other "trophy" body parts harvested from their foes. Inviders felt they should be the true rulers of Darkpyre and were furious that one of their own didn't sit on the High Throne.

The Avaritans, the Greed Demons, had the heads of sharks, sharp-edged yet corpulent bodies and wings like cockroaches, and tails like rats. Avaritans felt they should be the true rulers of Darkpyre and were furious that one of their own didn't sit on the High Throne.

The Luxers, the Lust Demons, were the only demons who were even remotely attractive in their demonic form. They had the feet and horns of goats, bat wings, snake tails, eight eyes and extra arms like spiders, but their torsos were exaggerations of a masculine, feminine, or hermaphrodite ideal. However, although the most humanoid even in their alter states, even then their "assets" were so overblown as to be grotesque. Also, their skin, although it looked shiny and appealing, was covered with sharp, toxic thorns, like a spider. The older they were, the more the arachnid features came to the fore. (The current Luxer Queen, an ancient, evil bitch, just looked like an enormous spider totting around on goat legs.) Luxers felt they should be the true rulers of Darkpyre, or, at the very least, the power *behind* the throne, and were furious that one of their own didn't sit on the High Throne, nor had the High King taken a Luxer spouse.

The final tribe, Prince Vass Glug'ulgros's own kind, were the Guliks, demons of Gluttony. The Guliks had vied with the Acedians for the lowest spot in pecking order for centuries, but recently, thanks to the brilliant malice of Vass's father King Xin Glug'ulgros, the Guliks finally clambered to the top of the hill. Xin had devoured—literally—his six rivals, set up puppets in their place, and now ruled as undisputed tyrant of Darkpyre.

Guliks in their demonic form possessed the head of a tusked pig, and a pig's trotters on their lower legs, three thoracic caterpillar claws jutting out from a jiggling, corpuscular torso crinkled like a caterpillar, faceted bug eyes, plus antenna and wings like a locust. They tended to be immensely fat.

Xin was all of that, but even more obese than ordinary Guliks. Also, in consuming his rivals, and many others, he had acquired their powers and some unique features. Instead of thoracic caterpillar claws issuing from the sides of his body, he had tentacles like a kraken. Sometimes screaming faces pressed from the inside of his folds of flesh, as if his victims were physically trying to tear themselves out of his body.

Through the ages, which tribe was ascendant changed, as they constantly vied for power. The struggle itself was the only constant.

Demons became more grotesque and animalistic as they aged over the centuries. Young demons like Vass didn't look as grotesque, even in their alter form. The younger demons had mostly humanoid bodies with mottled skin, horns, and wings, but had yet to develop the more distended, swollen features. The Kings represented one extreme of the anti-human ideal. Young demons weren't able to be much more than human even in their alter state. It was a mark of shame, although privately, Vass would much rather spend time with a lusty young Luxer nymphomaniac than an old spider-legged Luxer hag.

Right now, however, Vass was aware how unimpressive he looked, by demon standards: just a tall, muscular man with scarlet locust wings and hooved feet. He used to be able to manifest the head of a boar, but he couldn't bring himself to change his human face for an animal head, not since he'd been a full-blown pig. So he wore his human face, despite the fact it made him look weak in their eyes.

"I have solved the problem of feeding magic to the Tower in Arcana Glen," he announced without preamble. He knew what the plans of the demons and the Dark Triad were, even those plans his father had tried to keep secret. "I know where you can build it. And even the Guardians won't be able to attack you."

Vass outlined his plan. They laughed at him at first but after a while, his father bellowed, "This could work!"

All at once, the same foul creatures who had been mocking Vass and his proposal began to praise and applaud him. Sniveling sycophants.

"But you have only one last chance to prove yourself," added Xin the King of Gluttony. "If you fail again, I will finish what I started. I will turn you back into a pig, let the Hounds rip apart your body, and make you take a new birth. Needless to say, it will not be as my son."

~

His father escorted Vass into a chamber that he had never seen before. A huge, dark pit yawned like a black hole at the center of the roughly circular cavern. Chains stretched like tongues out of the Pit, lolling heavy on the rocky floor, thousands and thousands of heavy iron chains. Some of them were shiny and new, others were ancient and rusted into a blood orange.

"These are the chains that feed directly into the Infernal Machine," rasped King Glug'ulgros. "You might call them supply chains." He laughed at his own joke. His enormous belly jiggled when he laughed like an evil Santa Claus. "Up until now, even when you had your magic, you never took souls of the damned. You heard about it, but you probably had no idea how we did it."

That was true, but it was never a good idea to admit to ignorance. So Vass smiled knowingly as if he comprehended more than he did. It didn't fool his father one bit. But Glug'ulgros continued his instructions.

"Now you will be able to damn souls. I will give you all the powers of hell, not just my own power, but all seven sins. That way, whatever weakness your target has, you will be able to take advantage of it. Hold out to your arms and bow your head."

His father shackled an iron collar around his neck. The chain ran down into the darkness, where a deep growling like a beast or perhaps the grinding of machinery could be heard. Then Glug'ulgros attached more shackles to Vass's body, to his arms, his legs, one to his waist and another one...

"You can't be serious," Vass exclaimed, trying to back up.

"You've always wanted the power of Lust, where else do you think the chain must go?" demanded Glug'ulgros.

Reluctantly, Vass allowed the final humiliation to be set in place. He felt more like a prisoner than a king. And yet now that he was in this room, he could see that exactly the same seven kinds of chains were attached to his father. They also dangled down deep into the pit where the beast of a machine growled and seethed.

"Are you telling me that every King in Darkpyre, and the Demon Dukes as well, wear these seven chains?"

"Certainly not," said his father, "Only the most powerful demons wear all seven. For most of the ranking demons who gather the souls of the damned, one chain of vice is sufficient. If they are not matched to the sin of the soul they are trying to take, then another demon with the correct sin is sent in their place to chain the soul to the Infernal Machine. You have this power only because you're my son. I am taking a chance on you, to let you achieve greatness. That is why if you fail me, the penalty will be so much greater as well. I will make you suffer the tortures of every torture device in my domain. You will wish you had never been born in this or any other life."

Xin bared his stinking, yellow-toothed mouth in the mockery of a grin.

"But long before *I* torture you, the chains themselves will punish you if you fail to feed them. Behold, they are growing even now!"

As Vass watched, a second chain curled like an evil vine from the manacles on his body. Now he had a second empty manacle dangling at the end of a chain. One chain attached him to the machine in the pit, and the other one seemed to be waiting to be attached to another prisoner. The chains around him, those leading to the pit were old and heavy and rusted, but the only ones visible now are the new growths, shiny and silver.

As the new chains grew, a hunger and restlessness inside Vass also grew. This hunger was like his huger for the addictive food served in Darkpyre, food laced with Dark magic, which had a narcotic effect on arcanes.

But this need was *so much worse*.

It bludgeoned into a full migraine headache, and then spread into an ache that wracked his whole body. Every part of him felt buried in ice, then dipped in fire, then covered with stinging fire ants. It took all his will power not to weep like a baby in front of his father.

Vass growled at the King of Gluttony. "What have you done to me?"

"You have experienced the pain, now comes the pleasure." Xin grinned at him. On him, the expression was horrid to behold. The folds of his fleshy jowls piled up like sticky dough at the sides of a black maw lined with pointy, rotten teeth. "This is the good part. You will like it. You will like it a lot."

～

They left the room with the pit with the terrible cold at the edges and the sweltering boiling heat at the center. Vass thought he wouldn't be able to leave the chamber because he was attached to it by the chains, but as soon as he walked out into the hallway, the chains that bound him to the pit became invisible. He could still feel their weight, but even that was a psychic sensation, like a deep dread at the back of his mind, rather than a physical pinch of his flesh.

His father led him into a large, dark room. A number of frightened slaves knelt on the flagstone floor. It looked like a scene from a medieval dungeon. The pathetic slaves had been scrubbed clean, but they were scrawny and naked. They shivered with fear and cold.

Vass still shivered himself, with symptoms like the worst drug withdrawal ever. It was as if he craved everything at once. He wanted a hit, a drink, a f'ck, a meal, everything, RIGHT NOW. He was also exhausted and growing ever more so. The chains wanted *something* from him, *something* he wasn't giving them, and until he did, they tried to take it out of his own body. He could feel the chains draining his lifeforce, sucking out his energy, killing him painfully.

However, his father attached the chain that dangled from the manacle around Vass's neck to the neck of one of the slaves. As soon as it clamped around the man's neck, Vass felt the pull of the chain switch from him to the slave. Vass no longer experienced the pangs of hunger. Instead, he seemed to draw energy from the man attached to the chain, as if feeding on him.

One by one, the chains were attached to slaves, and the NEED that Vass experienced became the ability to FEED on those chained to him.

Next, more servants, not human prisoners but demons in livery uniforms, brought in huge piles of *things*—every indulgence and luxury imaginable. The hungry man that Vass had been feeding on now began to gobble down a huge feast. The man had to feed himself and Vass as well. The other slaves also began to indulge in every carnal delight imaginable. One started guzzling alcohol, another started shooting up, others indulged in subtler pleasures such as receiving the payment they had been promised in exchange for their souls, or revenge on hated enemies who were thrown at their feet to be kicked and beaten. Seven gorgeous women arrived to pleasure the man chained to Vass's manhood and Vass experienced every sensual pleasure that the slave did, including his climax.

Although the slaves experienced pleasure in the carnal and psychic rewards they were provided, Vass absorbed more of their energy than they possessed, and one by one, they died in the very throes of the ecstasies they experienced. However, the pleasure did not end for Vass. New slaves were brought into the chamber and attached to the ends of the chains in place of the dead ones.

On and on it went, until Vass himself could no longer handle the continuous high of what felt like repeated orgasms by every cell in his body. He blacked out from sheer overindulgence.

Eight

August 9, Tuesday
Waxing Gibbous

VASS WOKE up in his bed in his mansion on Earth feeling like hell.

He felt tired yet restless, hungry yet nauseated, twitchy and a little dizzy. His head pounded. It wasn't even dawn, yet the grey light coming through the window already seemed too bright. He was sweating and his heart was pounding for no reason. He wondered if he was going to vomit, but his stomach growled, empty and irritated.

He never remembered his dreams. Good or bad. But ever since he had been returned to his normal form, he always woke up very early in the morning, like now, before the sun, when the night still held sway, but he had no chance of getting back to sleep. His eyes snapped open, and he stared at his ceiling, living in a nightmare.

Every morning he had flashbacks to being a pig.

Fear. Pain. Hunger.

Fear again. Pain again. Hunger again.

Over and over.

No escape.

Thinking back on it, rage flooded Vass. But the rage had nowhere to go, because it was impossible to fight back against the King of Demons. Vass needed something to make him stop thinking about it, something to take away the pain and the shame.

That's when the living nightmare he always woke up to dovetailed with his headache from his hangover and his craving for another hit.

It wasn't even about feeling pleasure anymore, it was just to avoid the dark. That made him want to end himself. It was just to get through the day.

He needed it. He needed it so bad.

He suffered a wave of the extraordinary pain like he experienced when he first put on the chains in that pit in Darkpyre. When he looked down at the body, his body, he couldn't see any chains or manacles. He remembered the cold touch of the rusty metal against his flesh, even in the private places, but he couldn't feel it right now. However, the dim sense of dread at the back of his mind assured him that the chains were still there, attached directly to his spirit. They were invisible on his flesh, and yet they would control his flesh and make it hunger.

Speaking of hunger. He was hungry right now. He had other cravings as well. Every pleasure he experienced feeding on the slaves in hell, he now experienced as a craving. For the time being, it was something he could cope with, but how long before the craving became a driving need?

His father had told him that he would have to damn souls exactly the same way that a vampire had to feed on the blood of its victims. In fact, a vampire was only a shadow creation of the demons themselves, a human made into a pale imitation of the master monster that had invented and created it. Every vampire lineage had been founded by a demon with a chain attached directly to the Infernal Machine: the supply chain that must always feed supply into the Beast. Vass was now a part of that supply chain. He would only get his own fix if he took enough from humans around him for him to send on down into the darkness and the fire.

That was what he wanted, wasn't it? The chance to prove himself to his father. A chance to move up in the hierarchy of demons. A chance to move from being a pig to a prince to a king. He would make this terrible hunger serve him. It would be a reminder to never rest until he achieved what he wanted. He would never be assuaged with any merely physical pleasure any longer. Only the achievement of pure power would satisfy him now. Then he could enjoy all the carnal pleasures he ever wanted for the rest of eternity as a ruling King of Hell.

For now, though, he had to feed.

He pushed a little button next to his bed that summoned his servant.

Vass wasn't sure what the contemporary name was for the man who entered the room. A century or two ago he would've probably been called a valet or a squire...Maybe a page. Who cared? The point was that he only existed to serve.

"Come closer," said Vass. "What's your name? No, never mind, don't tell me, I don't care. Do you know what a vampire is?"

The man looked extremely wary, but also interested, almost intrigued. "I'm Yuri, boss. Vat can I get you?"

"I could make you into a vampire, Yuri. Or I could just feed on you until you die screaming. Which one do you prefer?"

"I'd rather not die screaming," the man said steadily. He didn't frighten easily; that was one reason Vass had hired him. Come to think of it, Vass *did* know his name, dammit. It was Yuri Lojka, that kid who... Remembering those details made it harder to think of Yuri as a piece of food rather than a person.

"Vat vould it mean if I become vampire?" asked Yuri.

"Exactly what you think. No sunlight. Blood diet. Would have to feed to live. Like me. You could choose to use restraint, or you could indulge. Like me. I would still be more powerful than you and you would still serve me and let me feed from you whenever I wished. I could still kill you anytime I want."

Yuri inclined his head. He understood a hierarchy of bullies perfectly. Like Vass, his main concern was climbing as high on the totem pole as he could before somebody snuffed him out completely.

"Do it, boss." By some instinct, Yuri knew to kneel by the bed and bow his head. He was a big muscular man, and the show of submission did not come naturally to him, which made it please Vass all the more. Vass reached out his hand. In a flash, his hand and fingers turned dark red, tipped with long black talons. Yuri's eyes widened, and he shifted backwards just a fraction of an inch as if he suddenly had doubts about this.

But it was far too late to back out now.

Vass closed his now immense, clawed hand around the man's neck, easily making a circle around the twenty inches of thick corded throat. As he symbolically closed a manacle around Yuri, Vass could hear the spirit chain lock into place. He was tempted to choke all seven chains around Yuri and feed completely from this one man, so he didn't have to use up any of his other servants. But he knew that would kill Yuri too quickly rather than transform him into an arcane.

So Vass only bound Yuri with one chain. And although he fed on Yuri, he also bit him and spit his own blood into the human, to give him some of his power and the resistance of his body. Otherwise, Vass would have used up all the man's energy in one feeding.

As it was Yuri screamed in terrible pain. He had to endure both the transformation and the feeding in the same session because Vass was too impatient to do it separately. Yuri soon blacked out, much as Vass had, but from agony, not bliss.

After the sun went down, the demon kicked his new vampire servant awake. The vampire had a distorted face, his eyes had become blood red and his fangs were bared with blood lust.

Vass threw a dozen warm blood bags at him.

"I know you want to hunt," said Vass, "But if you hunt now, you'll kill too many people, probably your own relatives first, and you'll draw attention. So until you have more control, this is how you'll feed. Don't leave the mansion or I'll kill you."

Yuri's eyes glowed deep red and it was hard to tell if he could understand anything that was said to him. He fell on the blood bags and guzzled them like an animal.

⌁

After Vass explained what he had in mind, John was very intrigued. The Ice Giant, Fallen Angel and Demon Prince were once again meeting on Vass's yacht. Vass explained his promise to acquire the land close to the building site which had the most leylines. In fact, the whole area was drenched with magic. Better yet, it was already shielded with a powerful spell that not even Guardians could break.

"My grandfather will be satisfied," John said. "It's a good plan."

Raziel was less certain. "It seems to me your whole plan has one weakness.

Everything depends on your ability to get the owner of Timber Falls to sell the land to you."

"That part is easy," said Vass. "All I have to do is find out what the owner wants, his hidden price, and offer it to him in exchange for his deed and his soul. In fact, once I own his soul, I will own his land even if I don't bother with the deed. I can leave it in his name, or have him sign it over to me or to John Helwall or to some other front."

"Don't you understand who owns that land?" asked Raziel incredulously. "I assumed you must. You even mentioned her earlier."

Vass was confused. "What are you talking about?"

"Naya Fairchild. The Dryad."

"She doesn't own a timber business, she's a tree hugger for damnation's sake. She doesn't cut down trees and sell them! Besides, she's a healer."

"Healing is just her hobby. She also makes pottery as a hobby. She's over three centuries old, older than you, Vass. She has accumulated a lot of skills in that time. But her main business is managing and maintaining the timber business called Timber Falls. She owns as much land as the whole Dragon clan put together. In terms of real estate, her net worth rivals the Magician's. In fact, she could be the richest woman in Arcana Glen if she wanted to be. She runs her business at barely a profit, however, so she doesn't make as much money as the Dragons or many other people in Arcana Glen. But not for lack of natural resources."

"How do you know all this?" asked John.

"I was the judge in a case involving infringements on her property," said Raziel —once Judge Renaci.

Vass was stunned. Not by her age or her wealth. He was stunned and horrified to realize his whole plan relied on enslaving and sending to hell the same woman who had healed him. The one he was so proud of himself for giving a truck instead of hurting her in exchange for saving him. It seemed like all his good intentions were worthless. He was going to have to hurt her after all.

The son of the Ice Giant was saying something, but Vass didn't even hear him. However, he jerked his head back up to the angel when Raziel said scathingly, "And you are never going to tempt her to sell her soul."

"That sounds like a challenge."

"You can think of it as a challenge if you want, Vass. You won't succeed."

"Everyone has weaknesses, Raziel."

"I'm sure that's true, but she's a good person. You don't even know what that means because I don't think you've ever met a single good person in your life."

"Hey," said John. "I'm a good person."

"Really?" Raziel became even more scathing. "You're helping your grandfather build a tower which will enable the demons of hell to conquer all the lower worlds and then storm the three higher worlds and rule the entire cosmos. They will enslave every single soul and create an eternity of torture and pain. But you think you're a good person?"

John's jaw worked and the vein in his temple throbbed.

"Oh, you didn't think it through, did you?" mocked Raziel softly.

"I don't like it any more than you do," protested John, "but I couldn't stop it any more than you or Vass could. It is what it is. The Dark Triad is going to win with or without me. I'm just a cog in the machine."

"Keep telling yourself that, John. Like I said, Vass," Raziel repeated, "You've never met a good person. You have no idea how to deal with one."

"I've met *you*, Raziel," said Vass. "You're a good person. And you still succumbed to temptation. Let me see, what was it? Oh yes, one of the classics. You screwed another man's wife. You sold your soul to have her. And then she betrayed you anyway."

Raziel looked away. His teeth were grinding but he didn't say anything.

"Never trust a woman," said John. "That's why I've never been chained myself to any female and never will."

Vass felt like a complete shit. Instead of thanking his friend for saving him, he only rubbed Raziel's nose in the mistake that had ruined his life. Vass massaged his temple. "My point is that everyone has a weakness. You did, and she will too."

"So you'll ruin her in order to get her land and build your precious tower," said Raziel. Derisively he added, "Do you think your daddy will finally love you after that, Vass?"

"F'ck off."

"Not that it will matter soon. I saw your new chains. Did you think you could hide them from me? You truly are one of them now. Soon that's all you care about. Feeding the machine."

Nine

‿

August 12, Friday
Full Moon

IT WAS NOW HALF-WAY into the month of August and Naya had been extremely busy with work. That was her reason she hadn't done anything about pursuing the Guardianship. However, when the Full Moon arrived and she had to face the fact she'd done nothing to answer the Call, guilt began to eat away at her. That unease motivated her to visit Sylvia's Pottery Yard. The Pottery Yard wasn't only her business, it was also her home. It was a slapdash shack that Syvia never bothered to fix up although she always claimed she wanted to. Most people never noticed the house or never realized it was a house. They just thought it was another of the mini storage sheds that haphazardly dotted the large yard.

What everyone noticed when they arrived at Sylvia's Pottery Yard was the welcoming arch between the trees that opened into a huge space, unexpected so high up on the mountain. And everywhere around that space there were stone works and ceramic pots. Sylvia's fellow artist and on-again/off-again bed friend was a Gargoyle named Gunner Ogoth, who was responsible for the works in stone. She was the potter who did all of the ceramics. They ran their business more like a commune for itinerant artists, so over the years other artists had come and gone. Right now, however it was just the two of them, though when Naya arrived, there was no sign of Gunner.

Naya checked the yard for Sylvia and finally found her under one of the outdoor canvas tents. The Faun was throwing a new pot on the wheel.

"I'll be with you in a minute," she told Naya.

Naya recognized the style as one of Sylvia's standard "commercial" bowls. Sylvia made sets of bowls and plates, using a glaze that was both safe to eat from and biodegradable. She sold these sets mostly over the Internet, but occasionally also to the hearty tourist who made it this far up the mountain to shop in person.

"I was wondering if you had done anything about applying for the Guardianship yet," said Sylvia.

"That was what I was going to come talk to you about. I haven't started yet..."

Before Naya could ask Sylvia about getting some clay and time at the wheel to throw a pot, Sylvia jumped to her feet and clapped her hands. She was so excited that she spontaneously switched to her Faun form. Her hair grew bushier, her breasts fuller and horns appeared at the top of her head like butterfly antenna. Her long multicolored maxi dress obscured her least favorite feature about her Faun shape, her hairy goat legs. Personally, Naya thought they were cute, and tried to convince Sylvia of that, but Sylvia would hear nothing of it. She did kick off her flip-flops now that she had hooves.

"Let me show you what I've done!" exclaimed Sylvia. "I figured you weren't really going to apply, so I decided at least one of us should."

Naya was taken aback.

"I did it!" Sylvia squealed loudly, an octave higher than her normal speech. "I did it, Naya! I made two matching urns last week, and I gathered the water that I thought would work for the spell I needed. I balanced the acidic with the basic waters, a mineral dense water for the Element of earth and a very clear icy water that I took from where it is still snowing on the mountains for the Elemental water."

Sylvia was skipping and bouncing with excitement. In contrast, Naya felt a deep heaviness in the pit of her stomach.

"I don't understand," Naya said leadenly. The truth was that she did understand, but she was reluctant to accept it.

"I did it! I applied for the Guardianship of Temperance!" squealed Sylvia. "Look at my urns. Aren't they beautiful?"

Naya had to admit that the matched set of urns were indeed extremely beautiful. One was a deep rich auburn that brought out the highlight of auburn in Sylvia's chestnut hair. The other was a pale, cool blue, like the icy peaks of the Rocky Mountains.

"So you already went to the Castle?" Naya asked.

"Yes! I met the Magician and his wife, the Fool. The High Priestess was there too! I think she calls herself the Seeress, but she didn't object when I called her the High Priestess. Her husband is not as bad as I expected considering he's the pastor of that silly church in town. In fact, everyone was fantastic so friendly and kind to me."

"Then you did it," Naya said slowly. "You're the one. You are the new Temperance."

"Not exactly. I applied. They haven't told me yet if I am chosen or not. I wasn't the only one you know. If you had gone when you first got the Calling, you wouldn't of found any competition, but now it's different. Now everyone thinks the Guardians are being chosen in order of the Thrones in the Temple of the Guardians, and everyone knows that it's the turn for Temperance. But the Magician told me flat out that actually they would accept any new Guardian as soon as he or she arrived and can prove him or herself to have the correct abilities for the position. You could have gone back in January, and they would have been thrilled to have you. I mean *I* could have too. But maybe I was only meant to go now, you know what I mean? Maybe it's Destiny!"

"You received the Calling?"

"Well, I don't know, I mean what does it mean?" Sylvia shrugged. "You told us that a waterfall told you. I was working on my pottery, and it suddenly occurred to me, why not? It wasn't exactly the voice of a river goddess, but it could be still the universe calling to me. Since you rejected your Call, I figured it was my turn."

And there it was. Naya did not think she had rejected her Call. True, she had been dithering. She had been undecided. She had taken time to weigh the opportunity. But had she rejected the Call?

By waiting, by letting the opportunity pass by her like a leaf on the river, apparently she had. Certainly, now that her best friend was interested in the position, Naya felt she couldn't possibly crush Sylvia's hopes by applying now.

～

August 12, Friday
Full Moon

About once a month, Posey and Naya drove down into town together to have dinner at one of the restaurants along Main Street. Many of the restaurants were run by Witches or Shifters who were their friends. This restaurant, *The Tasty Leaf,* which catered to vegetarians, was run by Electra Delarosa and her sister, Kalliope, scions of a Fire Witch clan. Many Fire Witches were excellent bakers. The place was busy.

Kalliope herself, wearing an apron and a hair net, came to take their order. Posey ordered a Golden Bowl: roasted sweet potatoes, chickpeas and brown rice, topped with carved radishes, carrots and yellow rosehips. Naya ordered an Emerald Bowl: adzuki beans, quinoa, green beans, avocado, brussel sprouts, broccoli and green pumpkin pepitas, all drizzled in kale pesto sauce.

"What the hell?" Posey demanded that evening when they met in town. "Naya, I just spent an hour listening to Sylvia gush about how she thinks she's going to be the next Guardian of Temperance. What happened?"

"Sylvia applied for the Guardianship, that's what happened," Naya said evenly.

"What do you mean, Sylvia applied for the Guardianship?" Posey demanded. "Sylvia the Faun? You've *met Sylvia*, right? Do you see the problem?"

"You know that she loves pottery. She's perfect for the position. You should've seen her urns. They were real works of beauty, and I could feel very strong magic in them as well."

"I'm sure that's true," said Posey. "Because guess what, Sylvia's magic is Elemental Stone. And that makes her a fantastic potter, but it doesn't qualify her to be the Guardian of Temperance. She doesn't have any Elemental Water magic. But *you* do. Also, you're like three hundred years older than her. You have much more experience. And more power overall. Why are you letting her steal your dream?"

It was Friday on a Full Moon. The Tasty Leaf was only a hole in the wall restaurant, with tables outside during the summer. Naya and Posey had arrived early, and were seated inside, next to a window, but as the restaurant filled up, Naya wished they had requested a seat outside.

"How can I tell her that it's *my* dream and she can't have it?" Naya asked. "The position should go to whoever is best for it."

"Exactly, and that's obviously you."

"That's not obvious at all, Posey. She talked about how encouraging all of the other Guardians were. It sounds like they recognized her as the new Temperance."

"I thought she said that they haven't decided anything yet," Posey countered. "Sylvia admitted to me that there were hundreds of men and women who were in line to audition, all trying to find out if they were the next Temperance, including Seraphs!"

"That's right," said Naya. "Traditionally the position goes to an Angel. I don't know why I thought a Dryad would ever qualify."

"Why would you think a Faun can qualify but not a Dryad?"

"Perhaps neither of us will qualify," Naya admitted, "but if somebody else gets the position at least it won't be me that ruins Sylvia's dream!"

"You know darn tootin' well that the only reason Sylvia got the idea was because she heard it from you," said Posey. "Sure, it's her dream for this week. Next week she'll have a completely different dream. You know how she is. For you, it's different. You can't give up on something you've truly had your heart set on because Sylvia decided it was her flavor of the month. You have to be fair to yourself and not just to everyone else around you, Naya."

A waiter appeared with their food.

He was cute, in an emo way: tall and slender with a kind face and colorful hair. Faintly glowing runes appeared and disappeared on his flower-petal soft skin. He had long pointed ears, longer than Elf ears and further extended to the sides, which indicated he was probably from Autumndelle. He was probably either a Dryad, a Nymph or a Fairy. Posey beamed at him brightly; he winked at her.

Naya wished she were attracted to men like that, nice boys who obviously did not have huge hangups in life or broken souls that needed to be put back together like puzzle pieces which someone had mixed up with other puzzles and dropped on the floor. And then kicked into a fireplace, singed, and then handed to you with a note: "Fix it."

But Naya wasn't at all attracted to the pretty boy. Instead, a tingle ran down her back when the door of the restaurant opened, and a thug with full sleeve tattoos walked in.

There was a jagged energy that surrounded him that instantly attracted Naya's attention. She could tell there was something seriously wrong with this boy. He was probably the same age as their waiter, but he had seen a rougher life, and for some reason that attracted her mothering instinct. Or *some* instinct.

"No, Naya!" said Posey seeing the direction of Naya's gaze. "Just NO. Please don't go dumpster-diving for a boyfriend again. How many times are you going to break your heart? And then how many years is it going to take for you to recover again? For once, why don't you date someone who actually…"

Posey never got to finish because the thug came over to their table. He ignored Naya, and stared directly into Posey's eyes. He spoke with a guttural, foreign accent. "You. Girrrrl. Kom vit me outside. I vant to show you somet'ing."

Finally, he tossed Naya a contemptuous look. "I bring back your friend. Unless ve find something better to do."

Unlike Naya, Posey was not at all attracted to the mafia thug look, to tattoos, or to broken boys. Posey liked soft, artistic bards who expressed their angst through slam poetry.

That's why Naya was shocked when Posey stared at the brute with big eyes that seemed to become all pupil. Without saying a word, Posey rose from her seat and followed him obediently out of the restaurant.

The smear of dark magic that the interaction left behind was like a razor being dragged across Naya's skin. She also rose from her seat. The waiter was just returning with their iced tea, so Naya threw some bills on the table, murmuring, "If I'm not back, that should cover it."

She followed her friend out of the restaurant.

$\sim$

The thug had already taken Posey into an alley behind the restaurant. Since it was summer, it wasn't that dark out yet, but the thug had already maneuvered Posey up against the wall in the shadows. He stood very close to her. Naya could feel the itch of dark energy surrounding him, but no details about what he was doing, or what kind of powers he wielded. Naya wished that she had some psychic powers, but her abilities were all very earthy.

It was only long experience that enabled her to detect things like dark magic being used around her. Even now, it wasn't actually the dark magic itself that she could sense, but rather the recoil in the earth from the abuse of power, and the changes in the blood, the water of life, in response to a psychic manipulation. Those things she had learned to sense in order to protect herself from mages who used dark magic to manipulate the mind and soul directly.

When the thug went for Posey's neck, Naya finally recognized what he was.

A decade or two ago there had been a rash of Vampires across the nation. But it had been several years since Naya had seen one in Arcana Glen. However, there was no doubting what was happening when he bared his fangs and reached for Posey's throat.

"Leave her alone!" shouted Naya.

The Vampire looked up and growled at her. Its face was completely monstrous now. It must have been newly formed, and it looked like one of the strong ones, one that was created by a demon directly, or not very far removed from the original demon sire. Every Vampire lineage began with a true demon. The further the lineage grew from the original, the weaker the Vampires were. Vampires who were able to control their thirst, and even behave like civilized people, were usually very far down on the chain, with their hunger as well as their power proportionately weaker than the demon-spawned.

Posey took advantage of the break in his vampiric mesmerization to break free and run. But the Vampire now focused on Naya. He bore down on her and grabbed her neck with one hand. He lifted her into the air. Her feet kicked helplessly. She was stronger than she looked; she had all the strength of a huge aspen tree in her small human body. But she wasn't a fighter. She certainly couldn't go one-on-one against a freshly-spawned Vampire.

Suddenly a fast shape darted into the alley. With one hand, the new arrival pried the Vampire's fingers off her throat and with the other carefully lifted Naya out of the way to safety.

Her rescuer had moved so fast into the alley that she couldn't see his body but now that he stood still, she not only got a good look at him but recognized him. It was the man she had found injured in the woods. He had left her his truck and the awkward 'thank you' note. She was shocked to see he was still in Arcana Glen. Naya would have thought he'd have wanted to get as far away as possible by now.

Maybe he wasn't a victim of the secret military laboratory. Maybe he was a Vampire Hunter. Maybe he'd been injured hunting down the parasites, and he would remain in Arcana Glen to complete the job.

He was looking stronger and better than ever, as if he had amped up his muscles in the week since they had parted company.

He pummeled the Vampire repeatedly. "Didn't I tell you not to harm any humans?"

"But I didn't! One is a Fairy and the other is a Dryad!"

"I meant don't harm *any people at all*, you f*cking spit-for-brains!"

He kept the Vampire pinned whilst he repeatedly punched it in the face. He suddenly became cognizant of Naya staring at him in horror as he turned the Vampire into undead hamburger.

"You're lucky I don't want to kill you in front of a lady," he said roughly. He glanced at Naya, seemingly abashed that she had caught him involved in such violence.

"I'm sorry about this," he muttered. "I'll just take the trash out now."

He dragged the Vampire out of the alley.

Naya heard a sob from deeper within the alley and found her friend Posey cowering behind a large trashcan. She wrapped her arms around Posey.

"Naya, that creature almost... he almost... and when he called me, I was screaming inside, but I couldn't break free...!" Posey wept.

"You're okay, sweetheart, you're okay. Come back to my house and let me give you some healing water."

Ten

August 15, Monday
(First Time)

VASS WOKE up feeling like hell—hungry, hungover, hating life. The sun hadn't risen yet, but the grey light hurt his eyes. He stared at the ceiling, but his body shivered as he relived being a pig hunted by hounds while everyone laughed at his humiliation. He wanted to vomit. Weakness permeated his body.

He needed a hit of power.

"Vampire!" Vass shouted. "Get over here!"

The Vampire scrambled into the room and knelt before Vass. Taking his demon form, everything except the pig head, Vass drained lifeforce from the Vampire. When Vass was done, he shoved the thing aside, snarling, "Replenish yourself with blood from the fridge."

Vass felt strong and clear-headed again, ready to conquer the day. He snapped his hand and put on a dapper suit.

Raziel popped into the room with a flash of smoke, which stank of demonic brimstone because of his fallen state.

"Vass, why is there a Vampire in your house?" Raziel demanded.

"None of your business," said Vass.

"Is that how you're handling the cravings from the Chains? You know that's going to backfire, right?" Raziel asked.

Vass ignored that. "Today is the day I get the deed from the Dryad."

"How?"

"I don't know yet, but I will figure it out. It will be easy. I'm smarter than a tree-hugger."

"I don't see how."

"I'm smarter than you, too. You'll see. One day. That's all it will take."

~

August 15, Monday
(First Time)

On Monday morning, Naya met with her yard crew and her two lumberjack crews. Her yard crew was headed by Gunner Ogoth, the same Gargoyle who was Sylvia's roommate/on-and-off again lover. He didn't make enough money through his art, so he also worked for Naya in the lumberyard. He was strong, never complained, and everyone liked him, so she'd put him in charge of the yard. But more importantly, he was the one who oversaw the dry kiln. That was a critical portion of her business, drying out the wood planks after they had been sawed into shape. It was tricky work, especially since her kiln was about a century old, made of brick. The machinery ran on steam and hadn't noticed the arrival and departure of the 20th Century.

The crews were divided into a Wolf Crew and a Bear Crew. Probably she was breaking all sorts of employment laws by allowing them to segregate themselves like that, but with Shifters, it helped avoid bloodshed. They ran in packs, and they didn't get along with each other if they worked too closely together. Riley was the alpha of the Wolf Crew and Bran was the alpha of the Bear Crew.

"What's this about Gunner leaving?" Riley asked right off the bat.

"I don't know anything about Gunner leaving," Naya said.

Gunner was across the yard, so she walked over to him and asked him directly. To her dismay, he nodded his head.

He showed her a letter. It was written in a strange and beautiful calligraphy that she recognized as the Elven script of the Glamir of Autumndelle. Naya gasped.

"You're going into the Armed Forces?" she asked.

"You may have noticed there's a war going on," Gunner said laconically. "Now that the Gates are open again, I finally have a chance to help liberate our homeland. Autumndelle has been under the rule of the Winter Elves for nearly a decade. Don't you want Autumndelle to be free?"

Honestly, it had been three hundred years since Naya had been back to her home Sphere. The war had only a passing impact on her awareness. Of course, she had been aware when a flood of refugees from her homeland suddenly started arriving on Earth. Other than that, it didn't affect her.

"But you're not an Elf," she said stupidly.

"They are actively recruiting Gargoyles for the Air Force. It's important to me, Naya," he added gently. "I know it's hard for a peace-loving Dryad like you to understand. But sometimes we have to fight for what we want. Freedom is one of those things. I just can't be here knowing that the push for the liberation of my homeland is happening without me."

She glanced at the dry kiln. She felt stupid asking who was going to work it when he was talking about freedom and fighting and important things like that, but at the end of the day, who was going to dry the lumber? She gnawed her bottom lip with her teeth.

He answered the question she was too embarrassed to ask. "Look, I know it leaves you in a lurch, but I don't want to miss this opportunity. If I don't answer now, I might never get another chance, you know?"

She knew all too well.

"Go," she said, "Go with my blessing." She stood up on her tippy toes and kissed his forehead. "May the wind be in your hair, mushrooms under your feet and water in your belly. May you find peace at the end of your journey even though you go into the storm of war. Come out alive and come back safe and sound, Gunner. You will be sorely missed." She smiled. "And not just because I don't know where on earth I'm going to find another dry kiln operator."

~

Vass bypassed the shields around the timberlands by the simple expedient of hiking on foot. The shields did not recognize a solitary hiker as a threat. Or maybe the shield let him in because Naya had healed him once already. Fortunately, the shield couldn't seem to detect that he was a demon, or the seven chains of hunger that he bore.

It was a long walk, but he set out early so that he arrived at Naya's mill while it was still morning. She was gathered in the yard with a bunch of burly men, all of them magical in one way or another. He recognized the magic of each of them.

He was surprised they hadn't started work yet, but everyone seemed to be throwing some kind of impromptu goodbye party for one of the men, a big Gargoyle. Even though the Gargoyle was in human form right now, Vass could sense the strength of his Elemental Stone magic.

A ripple of annoyance went down Vass's back when Naya kissed the big Gargoyle. But she kissed him on the forehead which was a little strange if he was her boyfriend.

Thanks to the distraction, it took a while before the men in the yard noticed Vass standing by a big pile of uncut logs. A man with the swagger of an Alpha and the disposition of a Wolf sauntered over to Vass. He was polite but forceful.

"Can I help you, friend?" the Wolf asked.

Hmm, thought Vass, evaluating the Wolf's magic directly. No icy Wind magic here, but warm, earthy Stone magic lay at the foundation of the man's shifting ability. The man was a Werewolf not a Lycan. Perhaps that made sense, considering he was working for a Dryad.

Honestly, Vass had come up there with the intention of simply trying to make the most expedient offer first. He planned to write a disgustingly huge check and wave it in front of Naya. Most of the time, the simplest approach worked best, and not only with humans, but with arcanes. But as Vass watched, everyone was giving little speeches about how they were all part of a family from different parts of the cosmos, all from different Spheres and different species come together for a common project. He restrained his urge to vomit at all the supersaturated sweetness. He realized that probably writing a check was the last thing that was going to work.

However, it was also clear they were losing someone who did something important around the yard. That gave him another idea.

"I'm here to apply for a job." He jerked his chin at the Gargoyle. "I heard a rumor that you're losing someone, and I thought you might need a replacement."

The alpha visibly sniffed him. Vass laughed inside to see the puzzlement on the Demi-shifters face. *Can't quite work out what the hell I am?* Vass snickered to himself. *Nor will you until it's too late.*

"Are you a dry kiln operator?" The alpha asked.

Vass had no idea what the f'ck that was. He grinned and nodded enthusiastically. "That's right." He held out his hand to shake. "Name is Vassily, but you can call me Vass."

The other man shook his hand.

"My name is Riley," he said. "You can call me Riley. Come this way, I'll introduce you to Naya."

"We've already met."

This time, Riley snapped his head around. He glared at Vass, but even more importantly, Vass could detect the sin on him: lust, jealousy, anger. Interesting. The Werewolf had once been the Dryad's lover. Obviously, the tree girl was no wilting wallflower. The demon could also tell that the shifter was trying to figure out if he was currently sleeping with Naya. Vass smiled mysteriously, letting the Werewolf wonder and boil in his jealousy.

"Looks like we might already have your replacement, Gunner," said Riley. "Looks like your shoes weren't so hard to fill after all."

"You!" Naya exclaimed in surprise.

Riley scowled at the recognition on her face.

"So you do know him," said Riley.

"We've actually met twice now," Naya said. "And I still don't know your name."

Riley looked smug. Vass wanted to punch him. Instead, he introduced himself and pretended to learn her name for the first time. Of course, he had gone over a file with all the information about her while planning his mission.

"It's such a good fortune that you showed up when you did," she said. "How did you hear about the job?"

"You know how Shifters gossip," shrugged Vass.

"I don't know what to say," she said. "I was going to hold the job open for when Gunner returned."

The Gargoyle looked incredulous. "I'm going off to war, Naya. I have no idea how long I'll be gone or if I'll even be back."

"Don't talk like that!"

"I'll tell you what," said Vass. "If the gargoyle comes back, I'll gladly step aside."

"Why would you promise that?" demanded Riley, instantly suspicious, the paranoid bastard. "Don't you need this job?"

"I can use the money, sure," lied the demon. "But if I need to, I can find another job. I don't want to get in the way of a crew that seems like family."

That was the right thing to say. Naya beamed at him, and her face softened.

"Gunner is right," she said. "He is going to be gone a while. I'm sure he will come back, and there will always be a place for him here. But in the meantime, we do need to have someone operating the kiln."

"Then the job is mine?" Vass couldn't believe it was this easy.

It wasn't.

"Let's give it a week's trial," she hedged. "If you show me you know your business, then you're hired. And you'll be paid for the week you were on the job either way."

~

Naya couldn't stop the thrill that shimmied through her when she recognized Vass as the man she had healed, the man who had saved her from a Vampire attack. *He's back. I thought I would never see him again, but he's here.*

"I still have your truck," Naya told him. She looked at him curiously. He wasn't dressed for work in the forest. In fact, he was dressed in a nice pair of socks, dress shoes a button-down shirt and two-piece suit, as if he were going on a job interview. Suddenly she realized it from his point of view, that was what he must have expected.

"You didn't need to dress up to look for a job here," she said. She didn't add that he looked very sexy in his fancy suit. In fact, that suit looked too expensive for someone in his position. But then again, what did she know about clothes? Perhaps he bought his suit second hand, the way she bought her nicest dresses. There were so many rich people who passed through Arcana Glen, the second-hand store was filled with beautiful pieces with very little wear.

"Where are you staying?" she asked him. "Do you have a place yet or are you still in a hotel or with friends...?"

"Uh..." He looked wary again. "Does it matter?"

She put her hands on her hips. "Of course it matters, Vass. You have no place to stay, do you? I bet you were living out of your truck—and then you gave it to me. I'm giving it back, by the way."

"No way," he said at once. "That was a gift." A strange smile lit up his face and made him look younger and less severe. "For saving my life. Not many people would have done what you did. Not for a guy like me."

"And what's wrong with a guy like you?" she demanded.

He shrugged carelessly, but he wouldn't meet her eyes. Broken boy, she thought. Who screwed you up inside so that you think you are so valueless?

"I have an extra room," she said. "You can stay there until you can find something more permanent."

"You mean the room in your house where are you healed my leg?"

"It's the same. If I get a patient, I'll have to kick you out. Fair warning." She pretended to look stern, but she couldn't help with a twinkle in her eye.

He grinned back. "Fair warning. Aren't you afraid to have someone like me in your house?"

"Someone like you?" she challenged him again.

"You know. A stranger. A male stranger. Someone who might take advantage of a beautiful young woman staying on her own."

"Someone who might protect me if Vampires try to drain my blood."

A flush claimed his cheeks. "Yeah, about that. I'd appreciate it if you didn't tell anyone. I promise it won't happen again."

"What won't happen again? Vampires won't attack, or you won't be there to save me?"

"I assure you, Naya," he said darkly, "If anyone hurts you, I will be there."

A little shiver went down her back. She knew that look. She had seen it before and vowed never to fall for it again. But here she was, heels over head, like a barrel falling down the waterfall.

That look warned: I can save you from everyone but myself.

You are going to break my heart, broken boy.

 Eleven

August 15, Monday
(First Time)

AS SOON AS he was certain he was alone, Vass took out his cell phone. The service up here was terrible. He had to augment the pathetic human technology with a spell.

"Raziel," he whispered.

"Why are you whispering?"

"Why do you think? I don't want anyone to hear me. I'm here, and I have an in. I need everything you can tell me about something called dry kiln operations."

"Who are you going to burn in a dry kiln?" demanded Raziel.

"What? No one!"

"Who are you *threatening* to burn?"

"You're offending me, Raziel," declared Vass. "What do you take me for? I'm a demon not an ogre. I thought you knew me well enough to realize I am more subtle than that."

"What do you need to know about dry kilns for?"

"I just got a job. Operating one."

There was a long, long pause.

Suddenly, Raziel appeared in the woods next to Vass. Vass jumped, glanced around quickly to make sure no one could see them from the lumber yard, which wasn't that far away, and glared at the angel.

"What are you doing?" hissed Vass. "They can't be allowed to see either of us popping in and out of thin air. All of them are shifters or gentle woodland fae. They don't have the power of demons or angels to travel anywhere in the Sphere at the snap of their fingers."

"I had to come in person." Raziel shook the human phone. "This device malfunctioned. I thought I heard you say that you had *got a job.*"

"You heard right."

"You. Vassily, Prince of Darkpyre, son and heir of the Demon King of Gluttony, Master of the Feast in the Pit of Tartarus for untold eons of endlessly looped time—you—got a job."

"I've had jobs before, Raziel."

"Torturing starving prisoners by stuffing your face with food in front of them is not a job, Vassily. It's... it's an activity, I'll grant you that, but it's not a *job.*"

"Go be an ass on your own time. I'm in a rush. I told them I had to pee. They're going to wonder how much I drank if I don't get back soon. Tell me everything you know about operating a dry kiln in a lumber yard."

"I know it requires *actual labor*, Vass, so if this is your cover story, you might want to rethink it. What happened to showing up in a fancy suit and throwing money at Ms Fairchild?"

"You really think she would accept any amount of money to give up this place?"

"Hell, no."

"Neither do I. So I'm trying a different approach. It may take more time, but I'll find out Naya's weakness."

Raziel pressed his lips together.

"You *want* me to fail," accused Vass.

"I really don't," said Raziel quietly. "But I don't know what success is any longer."

"In this case, it starts with knowing what a dry kiln is. Which you still haven't told me."

"How in the Light did you convince them you were a lumberjack wearing that six-thousand-dollar suit?"

Leaves crunched in the woods.

"Great, they sent someone to look for me. Thanks for being completely useless," snapped Vass. "Get out of here before someone sees you."

～

"Vass? Are you out here?"

It was Riley. "We thought maybe you got lost, city slicker."

Vass turned around. He recalled Raziel's joke, and said, "I don't usually dress like this."

No, usually he dressed much better. When he was in Darkpyre, he wore outfits of dragon leather and spider silk, embossed with platinum and jewels, worth fifty of these cheap suits. And by human standards, this suit was considered expensive.

"I guess you didn't figure we'd put you to work on the first day," said Riley. "But I have some work clothes you can borrow."

Vass trailed Riley back to the yard, where the other shifters clustered around him.

The idea of wearing the clothes that had touched the sweat of the Shifter made

Vass want to shudder. But he had to act grateful. When Riley showed him a shed where he could change, Vass could no longer hold back his disgust.

They all caught his expression and chuckled. "You can change in the woods if you prefer."

"How about Naya's house?" It had taken him about five minutes to realize that her house was just downhill from the lumberyard. Her house was closer to the Water Mill than the lumberyard itself was. A huge tree created one wall of the building, a living wall, while the rest of the house was built from rounded river stones. Moss grew over the stones making even the rock seem alive. It was as if her house had grown organically from the earth itself, like a mushroom. It fit the beautiful Dryad perfectly.

"Let me give you a word of advice," said Riley. He bared his teeth. He let his canines show. "Every guy in the Timber Falls company would gladly give his life to stop Naya from getting so much is a papercut. You better watch yourself."

Vass smirked when Riley turned back around. But, without a better option, Vass changed clothes in the shed. He felt like an idiot when he emerged wearing scruffy jeans, a flannel shirt and second-hand boots that pinched.

They met back up with Naya. She nodded at Vass's clothes. "Much better."

Was he imagining the appreciative gleam in her eyes as she roved her gaze over him? If she though he looked good in jeans and flannel, just imagine how she'd react if he stripped for her and showed her his power-pumped, dark magic enhanced physical perfection! And just imagine what *she* looked like with no clothes....

Already she was back to business, talking about timber and logging and types of trees.

"It's mostly softwoods up here," she was saying when he brought his mind back from imagining her naked. She said something about the kiln that snapped him back to attention.

"Oh, yes," he said, not certain what he was agreeing to. Something about difficult woods in the kiln. "I can handle it."

"Exactly how many years of experience have you had?"

"A lot."

She didn't like the imprecision in his answer.

"Six," he decided. It was a nice demonic number.

"Gunner had over 20," she said. "But six is good. I can work with that. I hope you can handle our kiln... it's an older model. Brick, you know. They don't make them like they used to."

Vass tried to remember which of the sheds around the lumberyard he had seen that was made out of brick. Damn Raziel for not getting him any information about this job he had supposedly spent six years doing. All of the crews gathered around to watch. The guys had their arms crossed and if Vass heard correctly, were already taking bets on whether he would succeed or not.

At least he had identified the correct building because it was the one the crews congregated around. It was big—warehouse big—and it was made out of brick. It was kind of obvious in retrospect. It had wood stacked up in the front and in the back. The guys had to use a forklift to stack the wood inside. The machinery looked like a bizarre row of steam engines from the 19th Century all lined up along one side of the dry kiln.

How hard can it be to operate? he thought.

~

The explosion was probably seen as far as downtown Arcana Glen. Hell, they probably saw it in the Castle. Fortunately, the Wildfire Emergency Service, a crew of fire Elves, mostly, and a few Shifters, arrived quickly on the scene. They put out the fire that consumed most of the lumber in the yard and before it could spread further into the forest, but the kiln was completely ruined.

"That was amazing," Riley told Vass. "I have never seen anyone f*ck up so completely. You literally blew it up."

Riley addressed Vass, but Vass had eyes only for Naya.

Her expression sliced him like a knife.

She was... disappointed.

"Vass," said Naya. "You're fired. I was willing to give you a chance despite having no references. But no one messes around with *my crew* and *my business*. Nobody puts my people's lives in danger or risks setting fire to *my forest*. But worse..."

She crossed her arms. "*You lied to me.* You haven't had six years' experience. I don't think you've even had one year's experience."

~

"That went about as well as expected," smirked Raziel. He'd popped out of nowhere to walk next to Vass as he hiked home—back in his six-thousand-dollar suit, which had miraculously survived the explosion and fire, although it was dirty and singed. "Also, your Vampire escaped and tried to bite someone. I made a cage for him in the cellar and locked him up."

"I need to feed," said Vass. In fact, the cravings had been growing all morning. No wonder he had been so clumsy. He had a pounding headache, itchy eyes, and a dry mouth. How could he concentrate if all he could think about was the need for another feeding?

"It was bad enough when you were addicted to the hell-food," said Raziel. "Whatever those chains do, it's even worse. You shouldn't have put them on."

"I didn't have a f*cking choice, Raziel!" shouted Vass.

"You didn't have to go back to Darkpyre," Raziel insisted. "You didn't have to propose this plan to your father."

"I did if I want my rank as his heir restored!" said Vass.

"Can't wait to get back to feasting in Tantalus, is that it?" sneered Raziel.

Vass was about to snap back some snarky answer that would put the Fallen Angel in his place, but something at the back of his mind made Vass pause.

Tantalus. It was one of the tortures of Darkpyre that used a Sisyphus Engine— the demons' version of the *Merkevah*: a kind of Time Machine that could replay the last day. When Vass was first assigned to break the spirit of the Fallen Angel,

Tantalus was naturally the torture that the Gulik demons had tried first. The Pit of Tantalus looked fantastic at first, even to the victims. Designed to resemble a dance club, it was a dark rectangle filled flashing lights and blaring music, thronging with half-naked gorgeous young demons and demi-demons, all dancing, drinking, fornicating right on the dance floor or on the tables, and everywhere, in every fashion, feasting, snorting, and injecting dark magic. Delicious scents and the throb of the music enchanted the victims with cravings. But of course, if they gorged themselves, the dark magic in the substances made them hungrier, thirstier, and more desperate for satisfaction than before.

For those, like Raziel, who were too savvy to imbibe the dark magic, a simpler method of torture had to suffice. They were simply deprived of food for a month, and drink for three days, or however much was needed to bring their physical forms to the brink of death, and then locked in the room with partygoers. They were surrounded by drink and food but not allowed to eat anything.

And then that day was replayed over and over. Always the victims edged close to the brink of death, when suffering was most intense, never allowed the relief of extinction.

Raziel was one of those who refused to eat any food in Darkpyre, trying to starve himself to escape his servitude. Vass had no choice but to keep shoving Raziel through the Pit on Replay, just to keep the Fallen Angel from dying on Vass's shift. On the other hand, it wasn't all bad. Vass enjoyed the feasting. He stuffed himself every Replayed day, knowing at least he wouldn't get fat from his excess.

Six years had passed like that.

"When I think of Tantalus, I can't believe you made me go through that shit for six modder'fu'king years," Vass complained to Raziel. "You were so stubborn. Why wouldn't you just *eat*? If Chet hadn't arrived and stirred things up, I'd probably still be in that Pit, thanks to you!"

Raziel raised his eyebrows at this interpretation of history.

"But now I know what I have to do," said Vass. "Remember I told you I would have the Dryad's deed and the Dryad's soul by the end of the day? It's going to happen."

~

Vass snapped his fingers and returned to the gravel lot next to Naya's cottage. There, still gleaming like a giant chrome and steel monster, was Chet's Monster Truck.

The Chariot of Heaven.

Raziel appeared between Vass and the truck. Raziel glanced at the truck, then back at Vass.

"Don't do it, Vass," warned Raziel. "You'll only make it worse. Accept your failure and move on."

"You accept that *you're* a failure!" scoffed Vass. He manifested a single demon claw, yanked the mystical black feather out of the ether and pinched it with his power. The ethereal plume burned with strange, shadowy, silver and black flames.

The feather had once been part of Raziel's own wings, back when they were made of Light magic and not Dark. When he had sold his soul, he had surrendered the feather, which had become the key to his prison—and also a barb to torment him.

Raziel collapsed to his knees, teeth clenched, fighting the pain.

"Get out of my way," Vass said. "And I forbid you to tell anyone, especially Naya, what I'm doing. Even if you forget this day—which you will—you must obey that command."

Vass released his grip on the feather.

Raziel glared up at him. "You didn't have to do that."

"Apparently, I did. You're not my brother or my keeper or my guardian angel. You're my slave. Get the hell out of my way."

Raziel had no choice but to obey and watch as Vass climbed into the truck and pressed a button emblazoned with an hourglass.

Twelve

August 15, Monday
(2nd Repeat)

VASS WOKE up feeling like hell—hungry, hungover, hating life. Pig memories pounded his head. He also remembered torturing Raziel with the black feather right before restarting the day. He rolled over to the side of the bed and vomited.

The sun hadn't risen yet, but the gray light hurt his eyes. He needed a hit.

He summoned his Vampire, drained some lifeforce until he felt better, then kicked the thing out of the room.

Vass needed a plan. Getting a job—that was stupid. This time, he'd rely on his strength. He was a great cook. Combined with his magic to induce strong cravings and addictive food, he could use food to get what he wanted.

He'd go through the motions of getting the job and a place to stay with Naya so he had an excuse to cook her dinner.

Naya found that Riley had given Vass some more appropriate clothes. Thank the Light.

"Today is a crazy day," she said. "I know you didn't show up expecting any of this, you were obviously dressed for a more sedate interview. We'll let you settle in and start work tomorrow bright and early, okay? We keep a regular 40-hour work week here at Timber Falls.

"But today, if you're up for it, I'll drive you around the mountain side and let you take a peek at our whole operations. That will let you know what you're going to be a part of. We like to think of ourselves as more than just a company. We're family."

"Family, huh?" He snorted. "Why do strangers want to pretend they are a family? Family members are the worst. Dangerous, jealous, cruel. The first to stab you in the back. Why recreate that?"

He sounded so bitter that sadness flooded her. Naya had been wondering if Moxie was Vass's sister, but now Naya wasn't certain. Moxie said that she and her brother were raised in a laboratory. Was that a lie or was that what Vass thought of as his 'family'? Either way, if he thought that about family members, no wonder he didn't want to see his sister.

"Wow," said Naya. "You must have had a pretty terrible family."

"No, my family was great," he said, apparently unaware of the contradiction. He winked at her. "They treated me like a prince!"

Naya lifted her brows but didn't challenge him. Vass was a mystery to her. He was hiding great pain, but not only from her. He himself seemed unaware of it.

≈

All day, Vass successfully avoided having to use the dry kiln—the "demonstration" had been put off to Tuesday. By then, he'd be gone.

In the evening, Vass went on the offense.

As a Prince of Gluttony, the one thing he knew about was fine cuisine. He was going to cook her a meal that would land on her tongue like an orgasm.

He had the afternoon off because he didn't start work until Tuesday, so he spent the time shopping for a fancy meal. He bought steaks and all the spices. He started cooking while she was still out on the mountain. Apparently, she spent almost all day just roaming around, consulting with the crews and talking to the trees or whatever the hell it was she did. She had told him on the drive, but he hadn't paid much attention.

When she walked in, the delicious aroma of steak and a spicy wine sauce filled the cottage. He had set the table beautifully for two with candles.

Naya stopped and stared at him. "What is this?"

"Dinner."

"You didn't have to do that. You're a guest here until you find a permanent place to live. You don't have to cook."

"I wanted to." He held out the chair for her.

She shook her head. "I'm sweaty, I stink, I've been outside all day. I need to take a shower before I can eat, sorry. What is that... meat?" She said the word the way another person would say *worms*.

"It's steak," he said. He frowned. "Very expensive steak."

"I'm a vegan. And honestly, I'm not very hungry. Go ahead and eat without me."

"But... but..."

Vass had been feeding her cravings all day. She should be *starving*. She should be starving for *his food*.

"Doesn't it smell at all good?" An edge crept into his voice. "Aren't you hungry?"

"You know, I was, earlier. It was weird, but I had strange hankerings for food I

68

seldom eat," she admitted, "but I sipped some Elemental water and stood in the sun in my tree form. That always helps when I start getting weird cravings for junk food."

"Steak isn't junk food!"

"I get it!" she laughed. "You're an Animal Shifter, probably a carnivore, with a hearty appetite. But I'm a tree shifter." She grinned at him. "Water and light are tasty to me. To each their own taste, right?"

He ate his steak alone.

$\sim$

That night, when he returned to the mansion, Raziel confronted him.

"I discovered the Vampire you made when it escaped and murdered someone!" Raziel hissed. "I killed the vampire, but I can't bring back the murdered innocent!"

"You worry too much," Vass said. "I'll take care of it." He was barely paying attention because he wanted to feed before he re-started the Day with the Chariot. "Wait, you destroyed my Vampire? Damnit, Raziel!"

$\sim$

August 15, Monday
(27th Repeat)

Vass woke up feeling like hell—hungry, hungover, hating life.

He was now on the twenty-seventh "one day to get it done."

At least, he'd started to get more efficient. After he threw up, retching acid because he had nothing in his stomach, he summoned Raziel first, with the black feather already out so Raziel wouldn't give him any lip.

As soon as Raziel popped into the room, Vass snapped, "I made a Vampire. Build a cage for him in the cellar so he doesn't eat anyone. You aren't going to comment on it, because I already know you think I shouldn't have done it and I don't care."

Raziel eyed Vass warily. "The Chains are making you worse, Vassily. It's happening faster than I thought it would."

Vass clenched the feather and drove Raziel to his knees from the bolt of pain transmitted through the magic link.

"What did I say? I don't want to hear your opinion! Do you think I don't know the real reason you kiss up to me? You're envious of me! Just like Chet, that low-born worm. He thinks he's so great now that he's a Guardian! Screw him!"

"What does any of this have to do with Chet?" Raziel asked. His eyes narrowed. "Wait—you aren't using his Chariot, are you? Vass, that's dangerous—"

Vass squeezed the feather again. That shut up the Fallen Angel

"Do what I told you!" shouted Vass.

$\sim$

After another day avoiding the dry kiln, in the evening, Vass ate his steak alone.

Naya finally came out of her room, looking clean and fresh in a T-shirt and yoga pants. She took a pot of some kind of stew from the refrigerator and heated it up on the stove. It smelled good, but a little strange. She ate that ever since he'd given up trying to make her crave dark magic food.

His curiosity conquered his jealousy of the food she liked more than his cooking.

"What is it you're eating?" he asked.

"Mushroom stew."

"I thought that only existed in Minecraft."

She looked at him blankly.

"You've never heard of... It's a video game...Never mind."

"I'm not much into computers or any kind of media," she said apologetically. "I spend most of my time outdoors talking with the trees and the rivers."

"Do they talk back?" he asked sarcastically.

"Some of them never shut up." She smiled. "They don't call it a babbling brook for nothing."

They both laughed. It was the first time the conversation had gone well the whole night. Encouraged, he started to talk about places he had been and things he had done.

She was staring at him strangely. "You sure traveled a lot for someone who..."

"Someone who what?"

"I can't tell if you're lying about all the fancy schmancy places you've been and fancy cars and boats you supposedly own or if you're lying about needing this job. Because it doesn't make sense that both are true."

Vass realized his mistake. He had been trying so hard to impress her that he had started talking about his normal human cover, a rich and fabulous playboy on the international scene. But he was supposed to be the boy next door, who needed to earn a living by the sweat of his brow. Shit.

He decided to cover his mistake. It was time to make her a little jealous. If he could provoke her to envy, that might be the way to trap her.

"So I heard there's a Faun here named Sylvia who is not only gorgeous but is probably going to be the next Guardian of Temperance," Vass remarked innocently. Naya had mentioned this during one of the Repeat Days, and he had picked up a strange note in her voice. Naya was envious of her friend; Vass was certain of it. He could always taste a sin.

Indeed, the comment evoked an emotional reaction from Naya. She glanced down at her stew and stirred it slowly with her spoon. "I wish her the best."

It didn't sound very convincing.

"She's gorgeous too," he said. "I love a woman with huge tits. Yours are great too, don't get me wrong, but a little small. Sylvia, on the other hand... wow."

Naya made a non-committal grunt. Maybe she was upset or maybe she was just stirring her stew.

"Still," he went on slyly, "I bet a girl like that is a bit..."

He left it open for her to make a catty remark about how slutty her friend was.

Women loved to do that, cut each other down when the other one wasn't around. It was one of the best ways for a demon to entrap women's souls.

"It's really none of our business," said Naya evenly. "We have a big day tomorrow. Why don't we get some rest?"

~

August 15, Monday
(35th Repeat)

Naya had an old beat-up Chevy pick-up truck. She took the driver's seat. She was dressed like the guys in the crews, blue jeans and a plaid work shirt. She wore sensible sturdy boots. The outfit just looked a whole lot better on her. With her slim, toned body and honey hair, she could've made a burlap sack look sexy.

Vass slid into the passenger side and let her drive him around the mountain. She was giving him the grand tour because it was his "first day."

"In addition to the timber we grow here, there are some other businesses that I allow on my property."

"Your property?" He tried to sound surprised. "You own all of this?"

"Yes," she said. "I bought it back when land was quite cheap out here. Colorado wasn't even a state yet."

"Dryads must have very long lives."

"We are as old as our trees. I'm about the middle of the range for my kind. No sapling, But not ready for tinder wood yet." She chuckled. "I mark the trees that the crews clear. They clear the area around the tree to be felled, then bring the logs to the yard where they saw the planks."

"Riley is very protective of you," Vass noted. "Are you and he...?"

"We had something a long time ago, but that's over." She said it firmly.

"Is there someone else?"

"No," she said with a sad smile. "I think I'm destined to be single."

"Why would you say that? A woman like you surely has lots of guys interested."

"Let's say, I'm set in my ways. And I have a weakness for a certain type."

"What type is that?"

She gave him a strange look that made her eyes sparkle and her lips tug upward at the edges. "Wouldn't you like to know."

~

So far, all of his ploys had been a bust. He was as clumsy as a demon on his first day on Earth. This was pathetic. He decided to try seduction next. He had been hoping to employ lust from the start. If that turned out to be her weakness, he would be one happy demon.

She had blown out the candles and turned on the regular electric lights, ruining the soft mood he had hoped to create over dinner. But he employed a little magic and the electricity winked out.

Vass snaked his arm around her shoulders. "Don't worry," he said. "I'm right here."

"I better go check the breaker," she said.

"It's fine," he said. It was a blow to his pride, but he finally used some magic on her, to pump up her lust. Demon-induced lust used mind magic, which was not as effective as a love spell, but it usually did the job. He nuzzled her neck and kissed the soft spot just behind her ear.

"I've been thinking about you all day, Naya," he whispered.

Thanks to the chains given to him by his father, Vass knew his magic was stronger than ever. But it seemed to have no impact on her whatsoever. She plucked his arm from around her shoulders and returned his hand to him.

"Go to bed, Vass," she said firmly. "And I want you staying somewhere else by tomorrow night. Riley has agreed to let you stay with him until you find something permanent."

～

August 15, Monday
(41th Repeat)

"I don't understand, boss," the Vampire groveled. "You made me. Why von't you let me feed?"

Why indeed. If Vass fed on humans directly, he could allow the humans to indulge themselves in pleasure while he drank in their energy. The problem with that was that humans were so fragile. He'd go through them like a football player through power drinks.

By creating a Vampire to feed on instead of humans, Vass had made a single source to feed on over and over. But that only worked if the Vampire fed also—which, again, meant killing humans. Vass hadn't fixed the problem at all, only added middle management.

"If you kill humans—or arcanes—in the town, you'll draw attention to me," said Vass. "I made you what you are so that you would be strong and endure when I do this."

He didn't need to bite the creature to feed on the Vampire's energy. Vass sucked in the pain and shame and rage the creature felt as if it were the strongest proof alcohol. By feeding on the monster's suffering, Vass increased it, by guzzling the shame at what it had become, he increased its humiliation that it was nothing but a source of food for him.

Why not just take it all?

The Vampire would reset by the next Repeat Day anyhow.

Vass kept drinking its lifeforce greedily.

The thing writhed in pain like a pathetic worm and collapsed and withered into dust.

Dizzy with mind-numbing ecstasy, Vass stumbled back to his bed and passed out as well.

~

The sun was setting, but the light was still too bright.

Vass woke up aware that the entire day had passed, and he hadn't even bothered to try to get the deed from Naya.

How many Repeat Days had he gone through this same shit? How many days of failure and aggravation?

He was so sick of this shit.

Time to cut to the chase. It was time to turn to the almighty dollar. No one resisted the green-eyed demon. Vass wasn't one, but thanks to the power his father had gifted him, Vass could do as well as any Greed Demon.

He dressed in his most expensive suit and snapped himself to the edge of the shield. He had no choice but to walk from there, but by the closing of the shift, he arrived at the lumberyard.

Naya knew him only from their encounter in the woods, when she'd healed him, and their encounter outside the restaurant, when she had thanked him for saving her from a Vampire he'd created in the first place.

It should have been a clean reset, but he could swear that every time she met him on each successive Repeat Day, she seemed a smidgeon less friendly.

It was worse today, when he arrived at closing time.

"Excuse me, sir?" she said, stomping toward him. "This is private property... oh. It's you." But she didn't smile as she had when she first recognized him during the earlier Repeat Days. "Can I help you?"

"I know you're short a dry kiln operator," said Vass.

"Don't tell me *you're* a dry kiln operator," Naya said skeptically. She gave his fancy suit a once-over. "You look more like you'd make it explode and set the forest on fire."

The crews of Shifters, who had started to gathered around, all laughed at that.

Vass flushed. "Remember when you asked me if I was really rich and important or just another red-neck trash-nobody like the rest of you?"

Naya's eyes narrowed. "No, I don't remember asking you that."

Oops, another mistake. No matter, Vass was about to fix everything.

Riley repeated, "Red-neck trash-nobody? Why don't you tell us what you really think of us?"

Vass plowed on. "Lucky for you, I'm rich and important. So rich, in fact, that I can take this whole shithole off your hands."

To prove he wasn't bluffing, he wrote a check for three times what her entire property was worth. He could have bought the Magician's Castle for that price.

Naya pinched the check and studied it for a long moment. She showed it to Riley, who whistled.

Then, slowly and deliberately, she ripped up the check into tiny pieces.

"Thanks, Mr Rich and Important, but I don't want your money. I want you out of here and I never want to see you again. Oh, and take your damn truck!"

~

August 15, Monday
(41ˢᵗ Repeat)

A winning lottery ticket didn't work on her either.

"You don't have to work anymore!" Vass exclaimed, after he'd arranged for her to "find" the winning ticket.

"I like to work," Naya shrugged. "Riley, call that foundation that helps the orphaned arcane children. Tell them we'd like to make an anonymous donation."

⁓

August 15, Monday
(68ᵗʰ Repeat)

He tried the simplest thing last. He simply showed up at the lumberyard in his demon form and started killing one after another of Naya's friends in front of her.

"The killing only stops when you give me what I want!" he bellowed.

He manifested the face of a boar so she wouldn't recognize him as the man whose life she had saved. He'd spare her knowing that she had brought this upon herself.

Tears streamed down Naya's face. But she stood tall and unbowed.

"Kill me too, demon!" she commanded. "I will never give in to the likes of you!"

Vass couldn't believe the gall of the woman.

⁓

He Reset the day, but he had no idea what to try next.

He woke up hating life.

Thirteen

August 15, Monday
(69th Repeat)

"I **KNOW** that you are using the Chariot, Vass!" Raziel declared.

The Fallen Angel had showed up, uninvited, in Vass's mansion. It wasn't even dawn yet. Vass had a hangover, and the last thing he needed was Raziel shouting in his face.

"Lasty night," Raziel continued, "I had a dream that I had lived this day over and over. I've had that experience before. I had it in Darkpyre when you were torturing me in Tantalus. I had it when Chet was using the Chariot to fight the war in Summerland.

"I know that if it's gotten so bad that *I'm* having not just déjà vu, but dreams of reliving the same day, that you must have been using the Chariot over and over. How many days has it been? Tell me the truth!"

Instead of answering, Vass stumbled downstairs. Unfortunately, Raziel trailed him. Vass went to the sink and retched acid. He stared around, looking for the Vampire, needing a hit, but Vass didn't want to feed in front of Raziel. Vass gargled with water instead. His head pounded. "I'll tell you but only because I find it too amusing to keep to myself. 69. Nice number."

"It isn't funny. If I know you're using the Chariot, you can be certain that Chet does too. The Magician knows. All of the Guardians probably know right now."

"So what? They were already hunting me before. And no matter how quickly they figure it out, they still have only one day before I can start everything over again and get ahead of them once more."

"But why are you doing this?" demanded Raziel. "Why take the risk? The more you use the Chariot, the more you will draw their attention. Soon they will be doing nothing else on this day but seeking to find you and stop you."

"I have to use it to get the land that I promised my father. Do you think that if I had taken 69 days in the real universe that he would have been waiting patiently for me to finish the job? Of course not! We would've missed the deadline by now. We have to have this done before Halloween."

Raziel jerked his head sharply, like an eagle spotting pray. "Halloween? Is that the deadline? Is that when the Tower will be complete?"

"Don't worry about details that don't concern you! The point is that I don't have months and months, but it's taking me longer than I thought to figure out how to get around the Dryad. She's very stubborn."

"I hope this isn't really about you trying to figure out a way into her pants."

"Give me some credit. That's just a side quest."

The Fallen Angel rolled his eyes. "Are you even using the Chariot wisely? The Chariot isn't like that knock-off Sisyphus Engine you use in Tantalus, you know. The Sisyphus Engine has only one design—to prolong suffering. But purpose of the Chariot, even when Chet use it, is to *learn* something. When Chet repeated a day, he studied his mistakes systematically, scientifically, isolating different actions so he could find out how to improve his performance. Are you doing that?"

Vass yawned. "Sure."

"Or are you just using the Chariot as a bludgeon?" asked Raziel suspiciously, "Repeating the same wrong thing over and over?"

That sounded more like what Vass had been doing. Yeah, sure, he was *trying* to 'study' his mistakes, but without all the work. Basically, he would try to lure Naya with one sin over and over, until Vass himself was sick of it. Then he'd repeat another sin over and over until he was bored of that one. Boredom more than strategy drove him to change his tactics after repeating the same failure ad nauseum.

"I'll figure it out sooner or later," Vass shrugged. He rubbed his head. He wished the damn day didn't always start with nausea and a hammer to his head. He needed a hit.

Finally, Raziel heaved a deep sigh. "If I can't talk you out of it, then at least take me with you. I know that if I'm in the Chariot too, I will remember the day even after you Reset it. By the Light, don't go through this time-wrenching experience all alone. You of all people should know how lonely it gets when you remember days that never happened for anyone else. Take me with you. Then you can discuss what you've done wrong and what you're going to try next time with somebody."

"What, now you suddenly want to help me? Don't pretend you want to help my people win this war. I've known from the start that you hate everything about what we are forcing you to do. You wouldn't do it at all if I didn't have your feather."

"I gave more than a feather. I gave my word."

"So what? You gave your word to Michael when he was the leader of your legion. If you broke your word to him, you would break it to us. In a heartbeat. Do you deny it?"

Raziel looked down at the floor and shook his head.

"Or maybe..." Vass kept pushing; he couldn't help himself. "You would only break your word to get a piece of tail. But not to save the whole Tree of Worlds from us evil demons. One day I hope to meet this woman who is so amazing she convinced the Badass Nemesis Angel to switch sides. She must've been one hell of a good f—"

Without warning, Raziel flew at him, and, with one hand, pinned his throat against the wall, and with the other, dug into Vass's chest with a spirit hand and yanked out his heart. It wasn't his physical heart that the Nemesis Angel grasped, but the core of his soul, all of his memories and thoughts and emotions tangled in a night of sparks and shadows.

"I've seen exactly what you really are," Raziel hissed. "Not the mask you show your father and everyone else. Your real core. I know exactly how much dirt is in there and also everything else you hide. *You can't hide it from me.*"

It hurt like hell. Vass responded by grabbing the black feather out of the ether, the key to the Fallen Angel's chains.

"Put it back!" commanded Vass. He crushed his fist around the feather.

It pleased him to see pain ripple over Raziel's face, as strong as the pain that came from having your heart ripped out. The Angel put the heart back and stumbled backwards, gasping until Vass released his grip on the feather.

"That's right!" Vass bellowed. "Don't forget you're my bitch! I may not be able to see your heart, or weigh it against a feather, but I've seen what you've done with yourself. You ruined your life over a worthless woman, and now you serve people you hate, including me. Well, too bad. You are weak and pathetic. You deserve what happened to you. Don't ever make the mistake of thinking that we are friends. You thought you could win me over with a few sycophantic actions, but I see right through you. You just want to use me, but I will use you first, and when I'm done, I'll throw you away along with all the other slaves who have already served their purpose. Like a piece of trash. I despise you!"

All Raziel did was look up at him, but the emptiness there struck him like a bolt.

"You're right…" Raziel said slowly. "I make the universe worse by existing. I should have faced this truth a long time ago."

Once again, Vass had gone too far and didn't know how to take it back.

No. That was wrong. Vass already had the perfect way to take it back.

He broke into a grin. "Fortunately, you're not going to remember any of this tomorrow."

"You're wrong," said Raziel. "Your toy Time Machine doesn't erase *everything*. The conscious memory is gone, but everything you do is etched on the hearts of those around you. I won't remember your words, but I will always remember what you really think of me. You put the truth out there and you can't just take it back."

"You're wrong," said Vass confidently. "I'm going to restart the day right now and none of this is ever going to happen."

~

August 15, Monday
(70th Repeat)

Naya was wondering how she would replace Gunner. That's when she noticed him: the man she had met twice, once when she found him injured in the woods and healed him, and once when he saved her from the vampire.

He staggered into the lumberyard as if he had been running all the way from the shield.

His face was contorted now into a strange expression.

"Please," he said, "I need your help. It's a friend of mine. He was attacked by a vampire. I need you to heal him. He's so weak... I couldn't even move him. Hold my hand."

She responded to the urgency in his voice and put her hand in his. She was shocked when suddenly she felt the air pressure change around her and they suddenly arrived in a fancy mountain mansion at a higher elevation than they had been seconds before.

"How did you do that?" Naya asked.

"I'm a demon. I can do that."

She gasped but he gave her no time to wrestle with the implications of his revelation. He pressed on quickly, "But you don't have to help *me*, you have to help an angel. Someone who actually deserves your healing. I'll show you.

She followed him downstairs into a cellar where a cage had been set up against one wall. There was nothing in the cage but a pile of dust. Outside the cage a man lay prone, his arm still falling inside the cage with the bite mark from two fangs showing prominently. The entire body was desiccated, completely drained of blood.

"He was drained by a vampire!" Naya cried. "You had a vampire in the cage. And now he's dust..."

"Yes. I killed the vampire as soon as I found him feasting on the angel but ... Obviously he had already drained so much blood... Can you save him?"

She knelt by the body and felt for a pulse, but she had already known the moment she entered the room that the angel was dead. Not even her healing powers could resurrect a body with no blood.

"The vampire was able to hypnotize an angel?" She was trying to make sense of what she was seeing.

"Can you save him?"

She looked up, her face stricken. "No. He's dead."

"I killed him," he said, sounding hollow. He leaned up against the wall and then sagged down to the ground, burying his head on his knees.

"You didn't kill him," she said gently. "You took the vampire off the streets for the safety of everyone. And you had him caged, which is the right thing to have done. It's not your fault the angel wandered in here and was hypnotized."

"But it *was* my fault. Ask yourself this: could an angel be fooled by a vampire?"

"Usually, a vampire would not have been strong enough to hypnotize an angel. And yet, the angel put his arm inside the cage..."

"He warned me yesterday," the demon said. "I can see that now. He even said it flat out: *I make the universe worse by existing.* He warned me, but instead of listening to what he was trying to say, I told him that he was a piece of trash. I told him... Such terrible things. I'm not a good person, Naya. The man saved my life, and I should've thanked him for that, but instead I told him he made the universe worse. So... he tried to make it better."

"I'm sorry I can't help you," she said quietly.

He gave her a strange look. "Oh, you could help me if you would only... Never mind that now. I'll worry about *that* on another try. Right now, I need to know—what could I have done to stop this? I'm stupid about things like this. I'm better at torturing people than trying to make them feel better. But you're really good at making people feel better. Not just physically, but emotionally. If you had been me, what would you have done if you were afraid your friend would kill himself?"

"Depends on the person, but often, if someone is in so much pain they aren't willing to live for themselves, they still might be willing to live for others who need them."

"Honestly, though, why would he give a shit if assholes need him? He should be glad to let them all go to hell."

"If he killed himself as a way of taking revenge, you might be right. Like I said, it depends on what kind of person he was. You know that better than me if he was your friend." She looked at him a little uncertainly. "*Was* he your friend?"

"We weren't lovers, if that's what you're thinking. I like boobs."

"It's okay to have friendship without sex. There are many kinds of affection."

"Please, don't make me vomit. Demons don't have friends. We have enemies and enemies with benefits. That's it."

What a bleak world he lived in, Naya thought. "And what category do I fall into?"

"So far? The first category, but I'm hoping we can move into the second."

"But now you've warned me that you're a demon," she reminded him gently. "By telling me the truth, you insured neither of those are likely to happen. Perhaps only real friendship... Or friendship with benefits... is possible now."

"Sorry," he said. "I can't let this day stand. Not like this. But I'm going to think about your advice. I guess I have nothing to lose by trying it."

Fourteen

August 15, Monday
(71ᵗʰ Repeat)

"WAKE UP, RAZIEL!" Vass commanded. "I need you!"

Raziel jerked awake and glared at Vass. "What the hell, Vass?"

"Don't pretend you were having a sweet dream," mocked Vass. "You were dreaming of the same day over and over."

The yacht rocked gently on the lake, although the boat was moored at dock. The sun was up. Vass had a headache, and the light was too bright, in part because he hadn't had time to do more with Yuri than lock the Vampire up in the cellar before Vass left to find Raziel.

I can make it through one day without a hit, Vass told himself. Just one day.

He knew he would survive because yesterday—not really yesterday, but the previous Repeat of August 15—he had been so upset finding Raziel dead that Vass had immediately killed Yuri without feeding first.

"How did you..." Raziel narrowed his eyes. "You've been using Chet's truck."

"I have. Seventy-one times now. And every time, I've screwed up. Also, I made a Vampire. He's in my cellar. Don't let him drink you."

Raziel reacted subtly.

"Ah, f'ck. You dreamt about the Vampire, didn't you?"

"It wasn't a dream, was it?" demanded Raziel. "It really happened. There was truth in the dream that I should have faced a long time ago..." A bleak note edged his voice.

"The truth is that I don't know anything about operating a dry kiln," Vass interrupted. "You're going to help me learn. And from now on, you're going to repeat the days with me. I need someone to help figure out what's going wrong."

The bleakness dissipated. Raziel looked amused. "I can only imagine."

"I only blew up the kiln once."

Raziel laughed.

"Laugh your head off, Angel. It's not as easy as it looks. This time, you're going to tell me how to make the thing work."

"Me? Do I look like a lumberjack to you?"

"Hurry up," said Vass. "I have to be at the Timber Mill in fifteen minutes. Wear jeans and flannel. That's how they all dress."

~

It had been 71 subjective days since Vass had attempted to use the dry kiln.

It turned out that having Raziel nearby to witness his incompetence hadn't changed anything. For the second time (in the "same" day), Vass blew up the kiln and set fire to the forest.

~

August 15, Monday
(73th Repeat)

"How is this related to conquering the universe?" asked John.

"Trust me," said Vass.

"Says the demon," muttered John.

Raziel smirked. "If his highness the Prince of indulgence wants to learn an honest trade, we should encourage it."

John harrumphed.

The three arcanes, Demon, Fallen Angel and Ice Giant stood in front of an abandoned dry kiln in Idaho, which was the closest that Vass had been able to find to the antiquated model Naya used. It had been Raziel's idea to ask John for help, although they weren't telling him about the Chariot.

John had apparently taught himself every stage of mundane construction, from mining ores and chopping trees to designing blueprints and installing plumbing systems. He knew how to dry wood in a kiln.

Raziel had even suggested letting John take the job at the lumber mill, but Vass refused. He needed to be the one who got Naya to sign the papers.

"Okay, John," Vass said. "You're going to teach me how to operate this modder'f'ker like a pro."

"It might take more than one day," John said dubiously.

"I promise it won't take more than one day of *your* time," said Vass. "As for me, I have all the time in the world."

~

August 15, Monday
(77th Repeat)

Naya awakened from a strange dream. In it, she was listening in on a conversation between a demon and an angel. They were discussing her.

It was terribly important. She awakened sweating and anxious.

But all she could remember were wisps of the dream. The details faded.

An angel and a demon. But the demon had the face of an angel. He was gorgeous and familiar somehow. She *knew* him. She felt as if she had known him for months.

And he was dangerous. But after she woke up, she could not remember his name or his face.

~

August 15, Monday
(87th Repeat)

It only took a dozen or so Repeats to get the hang of the kiln. He was, after all, a demon, and quite adept at handling heat. When Vass thought of all the Repeats he'd wasted trying to avoid learning his job, he wanted to smash his head against the wall. How was he supposed to know that sometimes just *doing* the job was easier than *avoiding* the job?!

Vass was tired of screwing up.

"Pretend you're not Fallen," he told Raziel. "What advice would you give me?"

"Try the opposite of what you've been doing," said Raziel. "Take pride in your work not yourself, pay attention to the needs of others, don't backstab your coworkers, don't play games, just do the best you can at the job at hand. Don't take a hit from the vampire before you show up at work."

"But then I'll show up for my first day at work with a hangover."

"It's better than showing up high."

"I think I can do it. I only have to get through one day."

"Don't use the Chariot."

"Pick one or the other, Raz. I can't go without feeding the Infernal Machine without the Chariot."

"You're underestimating yourself."

"Raziel!"

"Fine, I know you won't agree to that. Try being honest."

"C'mon. That's as stupid as not using the Chariot. What am I going to tell her? 'Hello, I'm a demon, I need your land so my father, the King of Hell, can conquer the Tree of Worlds and enslave you. Also, I'd like to spend tonight in your bed making 'the beast with two backs.' You think she'll go for that?"

"No."

"I need to figure out the right lie. But I won't try to spin it right away. I'll just play it straight for a while, figure out her weaknesses. Then I'll strike."

~

August 15, Monday

(122ᵗʰ Repeat)

Naya awakened from a strange dream and a sense of déjà vu. Something was wrong, she couldn't identify what.

Was this anxiety because she had been given a Calling and ignored it?

The strange feeling clung to her all morning. When she found that she would be losing Gunner, she wondered if her unease came from a premonition that something terrible would happen to him in the war.

Then the handsome vampire-hunter showed up. Naya knew she had only met him twice before. She didn't even know his name. But as she watched him stroll toward her, wearing jeans and flannel, a confident smile on his handsome face, she felt as if she had known him a long time.

He was important. She just didn't know why.

She went to meet him half-way across the yard. "Let me guess," she said. "You're a dry kiln operator, miraculously showing up to save me."

His dark eyes sparkled, and a slow, sexy smile curled his lips.

~

August 15, Monday
(365ᵗʰ Repeat)

Vass had spent a full year, subjective time, working on this project, but admittedly, for about two thirds of that time, he hadn't been doing much to advance his scheme. Once he justified his Repeats with the notion that he was "gathering information," he wasn't in any hurry.

He spent this day the usual way. Making sure Yuri was locked up with a few blood bags to cheer him up, working his shift, avoiding a fight with Riley, eating mushroom stew with Naya in the evening. A simple day of hard work and simple pleasures. By the evening, when the need for a hit became overwhelming, Vass just went to the Chariot and Reset the day.

It was a far cry from the endless party in the Pit of Tantalus, but he wasn't in any rush now that he found his rhythm. Raziel had suggested more than once that Vass try to do it "for real." Let time march forward, do the job, cut the Chains. Defect to the Guardians, was the unspoken completion of that thought. But Raziel was a hypocrite. The Fallen Angel insisted that *he* couldn't ask for help from the Guardians, only Vass.

Tonight, after a year of Mondays, Vass had a visitor who arrived in his mansion in a puff of foul-smelling black smoke.

"Hello, son," said Xin Glu'ulgros, King of the Guliks, High King of Darkpyre.

"Dad," said Vass, hiding his alarm behind a cocky smile.

"I heard a rumor that you have a Chariot," said Xin. "Is it true?"

Vass laughed. "C'mon, Dad. If I had a Chariot and didn't turn it over to you, you would kill me."

Xin lashed out with his tentacles, grabbing Vass around the neck. "That's right, son. I would kill you slowly and horrifically. But don't think you can lie to me..."

Xin squeezed his son's throat and his mind simultaneously. For the first time, Vass drew on the true power of the Seven Chains he wore, to blank out everything from his thoughts but his hunger for power. Not even Xin could pierce that storm of chaotic emotion to pick out individual facts.

Furious, Xin settled for drinking Vass's lifeforce, the same way that Vass drained Yuri, or the Vampire drained blood from a mundane. Plunged into the darkness of despair as he felt all joy and hope leeched away and everything ugly and shameful bubbling up, Vass could only endure.

Xin threw Vass against the wall. "How long until you have what you promised me?"

"Soon," wheezed Vass, rubbing his neck. "Soon."

Mercifully, Xin disappeared as abruptly as he'd arrived.

And Raziel wants me to give up the Chains? Vass thought. They are the only thing that saved me. Without power, I'm nothing.

He went to the cellar and found the Vampire. Vass drained the thing until it turned to dust.

Fifteen

August 15, Monday
(366ᵗʰ Repeat)

NAYA COULDN'T BELIEVE how lucky she was to have found a replacement for Gunner on the very day she found out Gunner was leaving. In fact, the coincidence was a little bit too strong. She felt uneasy for some reason. She also had the strangest feeling, as if she had been in this very spot before thinking these very same thoughts. She shook her head to get rid of the cobwebs. It was too early in the morning on a Monday for such spooky thoughts.

Naya said to him, "If you're up for it, I'll give you a drive around Timber Falls." She blinked. "I just had the strangest feeling of..."

"Déjà vu!" They both said it at the same time

He nodded his head at the same time she did.

"Yes," he said, "I get that too sometimes. Weird, isn't it?"

She nodded, looking a little puzzled. They moved to her to pick-up truck.

On his way toward her pick-up truck, Vass accidentally (not accidentally) shoulder-bumped Riley. Vass had discovered quite by accident that the best way to take control of the day was not to let the real events head toward anything work related. Let's face it, work was not his strong suit. He had wasted all those practice days trying to learn how to use the stupid kiln when all along what he should've done was pick a fight with her ex-boyfriend... And deliberately lose.

Manipulation, deception, and lies. That was the demon way. He should never have strayed from the classics when it came to tricking a sucker out of her soul.

When he bumped Riley, which by itself was enough to usually start a brawl with any shifter, he also allowed just a whiff of swine to reach the sensitive nostrils of the Werewolf. Vass hadn't realized until it had happened accidentally the first time, that he still had an almost shapeshifter-like ability to access swine states of his body, a lingering remnant of the curse he had suffered. In this case, the key was not to shift completely, which he absolutely would never have done no matter what, but just to let Riley think he knew what kind of Animal Shifter Vass was.

Riley's nostrils flared and his head swiveled. His eyes bugged, then narrowed.

"Don't touch me, pig," snarled Riley.

Although she was all the way across the yard, Naya had a sense when her crews were about to lose control. She was already on her way across the yard with her hands on her hips to yell at them to behave. Vass didn't let her have a chance.

"What are you going to do about it?" he demanded in a low voice. Then pitched even lower, so that only Riley could hear his provocation, "And Naya should not have bedded you, you're not even a real Wolf Shifter."

Nothing pissed off a demi-shifter like comparing them to a "real" shifter. There was a reason that Pride was one of the seven deadly sins. Actually, honest pride in one's own hard work was not a sin. Sadly, because it would have made Vass's job around here a lot easier, justified pride in a job well-done didn't feed his chain at all. There was no hunger in real pride, pride that welled up from within; on the contrary, real pride felt satisfying, like a full belly after a healthy meal.

The real sin was Vainglory: that edgy, sensitive, insecure version of pride, that hunger for *outside* validation, a bottomless pit of craving for approval that could never be filled. Vainglory was an itch that could never be scratched, that nagging need to prove you were better than everyone else.

Fortunately, Riley had that in spades.

Riley hauled back and punched him across the jaw. Vass pretended to stagger and then hit him back. Immediately a circle formed around them of all the other Shifter and woodland arcanes, who were all cheering them on. Only Naya was shouting at them to cut it out, but her cry was drowned out by enthusiastic shouts of everyone else in the yard.

Speaking of pride, the next part was difficult for Vass, because he could've easily wiped the yard with every single Shifter here. With one hand tied behind his back. No, seriously. He could have easily defeated all of them without any arms at all, just using his magic. But that would reveal himself as a demon, so that was out.

Besides the purpose was not to win the fight but to win the sympathy of the Dryad. She liked taking care of injured creatures, so he figured out that the best way into her bed was to be injured and have her invite him there.

Throughout the fight, he kept losing and yet provoking Riley with enough dirty little tricks that the man finally lost control of his human side and switched into a Wolfen: a humanoid that was about nine feet tall, with fur all over an immensely muscular body and a wolf-like head and claws.

The Wolfman kept beating on Vass until finally Naya convinced enough of the others to drag Riley off him. Right now, Vass was down on the ground in the dirt bleeding pathetically. It looked a lot worse than it was.

When Naya demanded what Riley thought he was doing, and the man was finally able to control his emotions enough to switch back to human form, he was still so angry he could only sputter and coherently, "He's a damn pig!"

"Boar Shifter," Vass corrected. He staggered to his feet. The injuries were real and hurt like a modder'f'ker, but this part was very important.

All of the other Wolf Shifters started talking about how much they hated Boar Shifters and all about the rivalry between pigs and wolves in general. The more they tried to justify themselves, the more outraged that Naya became.

"You mean this fight was because of nothing but a shifter bigotry?" she demanded. "I don't care about your stupid rivalries! You know it doesn't matter here what kind of Shifter someone is. You should be ashamed of yourself, Riley Jefferson!"

"Come with me, Vass. I'll get you cleaned up inside the house. I guess you aren't going to be able to start work today after all."

~

By 11:30 that evening, Vass was in her bed, kissing her and taking off her clothes. He had done everything right.

Basically, he had lied his tongue off the entire day. The key, though, was finding the right lies. It had taken innumerable tries to figure out what she already believed about him so he could confirm her own misconceptions. He had discovered that she thought he was one of the Shifters who had been experimented on in the base nearby. That was perfect; he had been there many times, although, of course, not as a prisoner. He knew about the laboratories, although he had never even been down there. Still, he knew enough about it that he was able to convincingly describe the place and an unlikely escape. He loosely based his lies on the real story about the escape of Moxie Bridgestone and her mysterious brother, a Lion Shifter.

He shuddered and made himself cry.

She wrapped her arms around him to comfort him as he described the torture of his beloved sister at the hands of evil human scientist. The tug on her heartstrings was awesome.

He did have sisters in real life, just like he had a lot of brothers, but all of them were half siblings by other slave women his father had impregnated, and Vass had not grown up with them, never mind cared about them in any way. They were only rivals as far as he was concerned. But he knew that most people treasured these things called 'siblings' and cared about that bullshit, so crying about it worked perfectly to make Naya sympathize with him.

Once she had her arm around him, it was very easy to let a trickle of Lust magic swirl around the room and undermind her resistance. And here they were, making love on her bed.

Suddenly, while she was in the midst of lust, waiting for him to bring her to climax, he withdrew. She looked at him in a daze. Like any demon-induced lust, her need for him become as strong as the need for any hit from a drug.

"Get back here," she gushed and tried to pull him to her.

"I just thought of a way I could save my sister," he said. "If you were to

87

temporarily trade Timber Falls over to me, I could pretend to trade the deed for her life."

That made no sense, but Naya was under a haze of dark magic by now. "Come on," she muttered. "After you come back to bed, we'll find a way to save your sister. After we fu…"

"It would just be a trick," he reassured her. "Just a way to deceive them and then I would sign the papers back to you."

He already knew where she kept her important papers and had already placed them next to the bed for this moment. He handed her a stack of papers and a pen. "Just sign it over and then we can get back to kissing."

"I want to help you and your sister," she said seriously. "But I need to know that…"

"You're the greatest helper of anyone in all of Arcana Falls," Vass gushed. "In fact, you're the kindest person I've ever met in my life. The sweetest and most compassionate," he added. He twisted the knife. "*Most* women wouldn't do something like this. They would be more worried about losing their business and their incomes than helping someone."

Of course, this was a subtle jab at her pride, not a real appeal for help. He allowed some magic to tickle her Pride. This is what she was proud of, helping people, putting others needs before her own. It was a strange form of pride, but very common among so-called "good" people.

Vass had to laugh at Raziel saying that because she was a good person she wouldn't fall for his devilish tricks. There was no real difference between "good" and "evil," except what made you think you were better than other people.

Now, not only Naya's Lust, but her whole sense of self, her Vainglory, was wrapped up in signing the papers, but it *still* wasn't quite enough.

This next part had to be the most subtle of all. In fact, he didn't even say anything out loud. But she had no psychic abilities, so he was able to push a thought into her head so delicately that she mistook it for her own.

When the Guardians find out what I've done, they will reward me by making me the Guardian of Temperance. Then I won't need Timber Falls, because I'll have a new vocation anyway.

To reassure her fear, he also planted a vision of himself and his imaginary sister running Timber Galls exactly the same way that Naya would, with no changes at all to personnel or policies. In this fantasy, Naya would be able to change her life without really changing anything; she would be able to become a Guardian without abandoning Timber Falls, she would be able to fulfill her lust for him, which she wrapped in the fantasy of marriage, and she would prove that she was better than anyone else when it came to willingness to be self-sacrificing to save someone's life.

She signed the papers.

He didn't need to finish what they started in bed after that, because he'd got what he wanted, but he took her back to bed anyway for his own pleasure.

∼

"Where did the television come from?" Naya asked. She had not noticed it during their lovemaking.

Vass had taken it out of storage in the bottom of her closet.

"It's yours," he teased her. "You do, in fact, own a form of modern media. Granted, I haven't seen a TV this boxy in several decades." He chuckled.

"We don't get very good reception," warned Naya.

That was an understatement.

He was satiated for the time being. It felt good to f'ck someone himself rather than relying on someone to do it for him and only feed off their pleasure through the spirit chains. The association lasted longer, like warmth that permeated his entire body. But now he wanted to distract himself from an unpleasant feeling at the back of his head. He wasn't sure if it was the memory of how the chains still bound him to that Thing in the pit, or...

Guilt. Vass was puzzled. He couldn't possibly be feeling guilt, could he? Shame was something he was used to; it was a common weapon in hell. But guilt wasn't usually very useful. Guilt was a weapon he associated with the Other Side, something *they* used to prod their own victims into doing what they wanted. Really, he reminded himself there was no difference between himself and the angels. They both used manipulation of the emotions to get people to do what they thought was best.

Vass magically boosted the reception of her television so they could see something other than static and snow. But all he managed to come up with was a local television station that catered to arcanes. By using magic, he had inadvertently accessed the station which was invisible to humans.

"We have a new vampire nest in Arcana Glen," the reporter was saying seriously. "At least twenty-five children from Arcana Academy are dead ..."

"By the Light!" Naya sat up in bed. Horror was stamped all over her face.

What the actual f'ck. Staring at the carnage on the screen, Vass knew exactly which "nest of vampires" had rampaged. He couldn't understand what had drawn Yuri to the school until the names were read. One of the seniors was Irina Lojka, Yuri's own little sister. She wasn't at a distant boarding school after all—she was living right here in Arcana Glen. One of the perverse features of new Vampires was that they instinctively destroyed their own families first. The other children had just been in his path....

"This is the first Vampire attack in over a decade," the newscaster was saying. "The Guardians have vowed to hunt them down and find the demon responsible for starting the nest..."

A pounding headache, the familiar itch, the need, bit him hard. Vass needed a hit. And now this.

Vass had finally created a perfect day, and now the Vampire had f'cked everything up.

I have to remember every move I made today, he told himself. I have to do everything exactly the same except for one thing. I have to lock the stupid modder'f'cking Vampire up in the basement, so Yuri doesn't go on a rampage and kill twenty innocent people!

Then again, why should Vass care? He had what he wanted. He could move on from this day, give the papers to his father. Their team of lawyers would hold Naya to her contract whether she wanted it or not. She had not only signed over her deed to him, but her soul as well. She hadn't noticed that in all the papers he had handed her to add her signature to, but one thing Darkpyre didn't lack was lawyers. She wasn't getting out of either contract.

Next to him, she burst into tears.

"You don't even know any of them," he said to her impatiently.

She stared at him as if seeing him clearly for the first time that day. In fact, she was. Her genuine sorrow over the deaths had dispersed every last bit of magic he had released into the room. Her own magic was that powerful—but her clarity came too late.

She glanced down at the papers she had signed and then at her own naked body. Suddenly she scrambled from the bed.

"You're not a Shifter, are you?" she rasped. Fear, shame, and horror all reverberated in her voice. "You're a demon. You... Every single thing you told me was a lie. You tricked me!"

For some reason, her outrage, at this late hour, infuriated him. He switched to his demonic form, a corpulent pig-like worm with brown locust wings. The smoke curled around him smelling of sulfur and brimstone. He played with a ball of hellfire.

"That's right, and you had it coming because you made it so damn easy!" he mocked her. "You deserved it! You thought you were being so caring and compassionate, but all you cared about was proving yourself to be a righteous person. Thanks to your mindless lust and your desperate virtue signaling, I got everything I wanted. But, hey, at least you were a good lay!"

Vass had heard about the concept of shattering someone's soul into little broken pieces, but he had never seen it unfold in real time before. As he watched, he could see her soul shatter within her as she realized what she had done. She collapsed into a little pile on the ground with her hands over her face. She wasn't even crying anymore. She was past that. Her aura, once bright and golden like sunlight, tinged with blue and green like water and earth, now turned completely black with despair.

He returned to human form and walked outside. He put his hands on the outside of Chet's Monster truck.

Why did I do that? Why did I show her my True Form? It wasn't necessary, I already had everything I needed.

I can leave now.

I can give these papers to my father.

I can prove myself a worthy Heir of the King of Darkpyre. I will be a Prince again, feared and respected by all the lesser demons.

I shouldn't start the day over. It may not turn out as well for me.

But he climbed back into the truck and pushed the reset button.

Sixteen

August 15, Monday
(367ᵗʰ Repeat)

"HOW DID HE DO?" Naya inquired discretely of Riley at the end of the day.

"Well, you should talk to the guys in the yard but from what I could see, he was hard-working and confident and didn't boast about it. I think he'll fit in here. I hate to say it, given what kind of Shifter he is."

"What is that supposed to mean?"

"Nothing, just a suspicion. But it doesn't matter. It doesn't matter what kind of shifter anyone is, whether they're a full shifter or a demi-shifter. Just as long as the work gets done."

"That's right," she said. "Now try to remember that the next time we go to the bar."

Riley's grin turned lopsided. "It's one thing to convince me, it's another to convince my Wolfen."

After her guest and Naya had both showered in their separate bathrooms, they sat down together in her small dining room for dinner. She heated up the mushroom stew she had in the refrigerator.

"I'm sorry I don't have more food," she said.

"I am fine." Vass polished off the mushroom stew in about a minute and thirty seconds and then forlornly stared into his empty bowl.

She felt terrible she hadn't bought him something more substantial. Riley hadn't told her what kind of Shifter he was, but usually Shifters weren't vegetarian, as she was.

"Next time I'll buy you a steak," she joked.

Vass looked surprised. "I thought you didn't like the smell of meat in your kitchen."

"How did you know that?"

"You're a Dryad," he said, adding, as if it were common knowledge, "Aren't you vegan?"

"Yes, but..."

His stomach rumbled audibly.

"I can tell you need a little more to eat," she finished.

"I'm feeling something strange. It's like a craving for food but different than I felt before."

"Are you sick?"

"No... I think it's real hunger!"

"I definitely should've bought more food."

"You don't understand. I've never been *hungry* before. I haven't felt real, non-metaphorical *hunger*. I've craved food many times, but not because I actually *needed* it. I must've burned a lot of calories today. How weird."

"Listen," she said. She didn't want to intrude on his privacy, but she could only imagine what terrible things that happened to him in the past. However, if he had been a lab rat, perhaps hunger manipulation was one of the tortures they put him through. "I don't know what was done to you or what you experienced..."

"Naya," he cut her off, "I think you have the wrong impression about me. That suit I wore today was not a rental. I didn't have the hard luck life you seem to think I did. Just the opposite. My father may be an asshole, but he's an extremely wealthy asshole. Wealthy like you wouldn't even believe. I had everything I ever wanted growing up. Went to a private school. Terrible place, but expensive as hell. My whole life I've never had a real job, unless you count going to fancy parties and acting like a dick. That's been my entire life. Until now."

She stared at him. He was right; that was not the background she had imagined for him. Nonetheless, despite his claim that he "had everything he ever wanted growing up," she gathered he only meant materialistically. It didn't sound like his family or his school had provided his child-self any emotional support.

"What changed?" she asked quietly.

"I'm not going to accept any help from my father. On the contrary, he thinks I can't do this. This may sound like a cliché, but I have something to prove."

"So this is one of those situations where he wants to control your life and you want to prove you can do without him and his money?"

"Yeah, something like that. Look, if you want me to leave, I understand..."

"Vass," she said, "It isn't really any of my business why you took the job. I hope it wasn't because you think there might be something between us, because I'm not looking for a relationship and I want to be upfront with you about that. But as for what's between you and your father... Among Dryads, there's a saying: *No acorn can grow tall in the shadow of its parent tree.* That's why I came to the Mundane Sphere. I have a loving, caring family, but they were smothering me back in Autumndelle. Here I can be my own woman. Building this business, being part of this community... That means everything to me. I just hope you can find a way to build a life of your own, not in the shadow of anyone else. Stay here tonight, don't go home."

He flashed that rock star smile at her. "I can stay the night?"

She wagged her finger. "Just to sleep. The guys said you did a great job on the kiln. I would love to have you as long as you are willing to work here. I can't believe you did that well if this is really your first job. The guys all swear you must have had years of experience!"

"Sometimes it does feel like years," he said deprecatingly. "Sometimes it feels like I only found out what a dry kiln was just yesterday. I studied it hard before I came here. Thank you, Naya."

She leaned forward and kissed him on the cheek. It was a chaste, almost sisterly kiss. From the smoldering look he threw her, Naya could tell he wanted much more. But then he glanced away, cleared his throat, and said, "I'm going to get some shut eye."

~

This day was a complete bust, Vass thought, as he kicked off his shoes and lay down fully closed on his bed in Naya's spare room. Obviously, I'm going to have to start over again and go back to all the moves I made when I ended up getting her to sign the papers.

His stomach growled. He also felt a curious ache in his muscles. He had really thrown himself into the work today, and, man, he could feel it. Actual exhaustion. Like hunger, in his "real" life, he had only ever felt the tiredness that came after excessive indulgence and orgies and other such pleasures.

I'll go up to the truck as soon as she is asleep, he promised himself. For now, I'll just rest a little.

~

August 16, Tuesday Morning
(New Day)

What felt like a few moments later, he woke up, feeling heavenly. Except for his growling stomach—he was hungrier than ever—he felt curiously good. It was nice and rather strange not waking up with a hangover. Plus, the light in his room was soothing, bluish. And his bed...

Suddenly he leapt out of the single twin bed. He wasn't in his room in the mansion suffering a hangover, the way he was always supposed to begin his day when he had done a do-over. He was still in the guest room at Naya's cottage. He had fallen asleep last night and forgotten to go out to the truck.

Even the Chariot of Heaven had limits and it could not re-do more than 24 hours. If he tried to start to do over now, it would reset at a different place than he was used to, and he would mess everything up.

Crap, Vass thought. *I can't go back again. I have to go forward.*

Seventeen

August 17, Wednesday
(New Day)

NOW THAT SHE knew what to look for, Naya couldn't believe she'd failed to put the puzzle pieces together for so long. Vass displayed flashes of that coastal elite snobbery that she normally found insufferable. What made it bearable in Vass was that he was trying so hard to fit in with the others. For someone who claimed he had no work ethic, he worked very hard; for someone who claimed he had never done this job before, he showed competency and confidence that earned the respect of everyone on the team.

Getting on with the other Shifters was a little more difficult, but that was always true. All of the Wolves had a problem with him and vice versa. It wasn't personal. It seemed to be triggered by some smell, a pheromone issue. Fortunately, the wolf crew worked on the mountainside, whereas Vass worked in the yard. So, they didn't see each other except when they came in to get new machinery or drive in a load of logs.

Meanwhile, Naya realized she was a hypocrite. She could dish out great advice about standing up for yourself and doing something worthwhile with your life, but she had thrown away the Calling given to her. Sylvia was avoiding her, and Naya didn't know if it was because Sylvia had gotten news that she *was* the Guardian of Temperance, and she didn't want to hurt Naya's feelings, or Sylvia had bad news and she was too embarrassed to let her friends know she hadn't made it. Either way coldness between them bothered Naya. Here she had given up on her dream so as not to alienate her friend, and it seemed as though they were alienated from each other anyway.

Finally, Naya made up her mind to go ahead and create the two vases she would need if she were to apply for the Guardianship. As far as she knew, it could have already been given to someone else, maybe even Sylvia, but for her own sake, Naya decided she would still make the vases.

The Guardian of Temperance was the Keeper of the Waters from the Four Elemental Spheres: Autumndelle, Springvale, Winterdom and Summerland, each kind of water tilted toward the Elemental powers of Stone, Water, Wind and Fire. It might seem strange that there were "waters" associated with Elemental Fire or Elemental Earth, but everyone needed to drink, and the waters that came from each Sphere had slightly different kinds of magical properties. Mixing them was its own art form, and very important in healing. The Guardian of Temperance had to have two opposite Elemental powers. It didn't hurt if she had all four, but he or she had to have at least two. Naya had Stone and Water.

The two vases that she would create would be from the clay taken from two different Spheres, those she would connect if she were the Keeper of the Gates between them, Autumndelle and Springvale. From previous visits to those Spheres, she had both clay and water from each realm. She maintained her own reservoir, although it had dwindled since the closing of the Gates.

She usually preferred to use the potter's wheel at Sylvia's place, but she dragged hers out of storage and put it on the porch.

On a day when she finished her rounds early, she scheduled a block of time to work on her project. Since she was her own boss, she could do that if she wanted to. She would make up for any work she missed on the weekend. She worked seven days a week anyway. Sylvia accused her of being a workaholic. Naya didn't think she was a workaholic... She also enjoyed hobbies such as pottery. But in a sense, this was another kind of work, so maybe Sylvia was right. When you enjoyed something so much that you would not do anything else whether you were paid or not, was that work or play?

She didn't have a dedicated pottery room in her small cottage. Her only spare room was used for healing people, and besides she had a guest staying there now. Thinking of Vass reminded her of that afternoon, when she saw him remove his shirt and pour water over his head. The rivulets of water had traced the contours of his muscular chest. It had been quite an inspiring sight. She had to thank August for the kiss of heat that made him remove his shirt.

That was another good reason to sit on the porch of her cottage. From here, she could watch the workers in the timber yard. Often, large stacks of cut and uncut timber blocked them from her direct line of sight, but every now and then she would see Vass weaving in and out of the piles of wood. She had to drink up every moment with him, because he wouldn't be here long. He clearly had many other skills and resources. He didn't need this job, except to prove whatever obscure point he had to prove to his father.

Once Vass had realized he didn't need to prove anything to a man who had obviously never shown him an ounce of affection, Vass could move on. Probably he'd go on to be the CEO of some huge multinational company and become immensely wealthy in his own right. She was certain he was smart as a whip and could do anything he wanted. He wasn't rooted in one spot like she was. If she was Earth and Water, he was Fire and Wind: a blaze, billowing smoke; lightning from a thunderstorm. No, that wasn't quite right either. There was definitely an earthy element to him. He was certainly one who could appreciate the carnal pleasures of life.

She was still smoothing the clay on the second vase she had thrown on the wheel when he came home from his shift. It was still bright outside, so she was surprised that it was already past five. Instead of going inside, he sat on the steps next to her. He sniffed his armpit. "I hope I don't stink too much."

"All I can smell is the clay," she said. Actually, that wasn't true. She was very aware of his scent, but it didn't smell bad to her. He smelled like masculine sweat, like something smoky, delicious, and dangerous.

"I didn't know you could make such beautiful things out of clay," he said wonderingly. "Even after all this time, there are still things I am discovering about you.""

"Even after all this time? You haven't even worked for me for one full week. You're still on probation," she teased.

"That's funny," he said with a grin. "Feels like it's been months. Are the pots for anything in particular or do you just enjoy making them?"

She was silent for a long time. She wasn't sure how much to tell him. She felt embarrassed about what she had done, and what she has failed to do.

"These are tools you need to apply for the Guardianship of Temperance, aren't they?"

"How could you possibly know about that?" she asked.

"You mentioned it, on the first day. When you drove me around in your pick-up truck, giving me a tour of all of Timber Falls."

"But I never did that. You went to work right away, remember?"

"Oh. Right."

She wrinkled her brow, seeking the memory. She remembered that first day he went to work for her very well. Yet she had a nagging feeling that the event he described had happened too, although it didn't feel completely real. It was like something that had happened in a dream.

"Sometimes I have dreams where I live my entire day, think I wake up, but discover that I have to start the same day over again, that it hasn't even started yet," she remarked, "Sometimes I even feel as if I've lived the same day over and over, with strange little differences. Do you ever feel like that?"

"All the time!" Vass said. "I mean, I used to feel like that a lot. But hopefully not so much anymore. Anyway, however I heard about the Guardianship, I think you should go for it."

"Because I also have something to prove?"

"No, Naya, you don't have to prove anything to anybody. You should go for it because it truly is your Calling."

~

One minute, Vass was sitting on the porch next to Naya, impressed with himself because he was having a conversation with her like a mature, decent normal human being. The next thing he knew, he was staring at her not as a person or even as a desirable woman, but as a source of energy. His hand began to tremble, and he thought about how much he craved a feeding.

What was going on? He felt hot and itchy, his hands trembled, a nervous tic made his eye wink. His erratic thoughts veered into fantasies of draining the life force out of those around him... he recognized the symptoms, but why now?! He had gotten his cravings under control and not suffered any symptoms like this in months...

No. All the blood drained from his face. *It hasn't been months.* It was just like he told her; it *felt* like months to him. Months *had* passed for him.

But to everyone else it was just a few days. Everything he had achieved was just an illusion. He felt like he was controlling his cravings because he was just reliving the same day over and over, so the cravings never got any worse.

Since he had terrified Naya by revealing his true form, and then overslept the next day, he had decided to try a different approach. He wouldn't use the Chariot of Heaven anymore. He wouldn't keep reliving the same day. He would force himself to go forward, one new day at a time.

And look where that got him. He was shaking like the last leaf of autumn in the first big winter storm. He had lost track of whatever she was saying and was staring at her wondering how much a Dryad could give him in lifeforce. He wanted to chain her and drain her. He quivered with the need to feed.

"I'm tired," he said abruptly. "I'm going to bed. I don't need dinner."

She looked at him bewildered and hurt. He couldn't explain that this was for the best. He stormed into the cottage and into the spare room. He slammed the door. He tried to lock it, but there was no lock. He sat down against the door, wrapping his knees in his arms. His whole body was shaking now.

F'ck this. F'ck f'ck f'ck.

Wait. Why was he panicking? He still had Yuri, his pet vampire, back in the cage at his mansion. Perfect. He would feed on Yuri and then come back here. Maybe he could even join Naya for dinner like a civilized person after he settled his craving.

～

Yuri was a brave man and he resisted as long as he could before he started screaming. By the time that Vass felt satiated enough to release him, the strong and proud man was nothing but a pile of skin and bones sobbing in a corner of the cage.

Out of some perverse curiosity, Vass stayed in the root cellar, sitting on a small stool, watching his victim crawl around the cage trying to recover. Vass told himself that he only wanted to know if the Vampire would survive the feeding. Try as he might to restrain himself, Vass had taken more lifeforce from the Vampire than he had intended.

Vass had seven chains attached to him that he needed to siphon energy through himself and down into the Infernal Machine. He needed to feed from seven souls every 24 hours, or the Infernal Machine would start to drain his own life energy. He should've stuck to his original plan to make some more vampires.

But his root cellar wasn't that big. He would have to enlarge it. And get more cages.

So much for his pretense at being a mature, decent, normal human being.

Echoing his own dark thoughts, Yuri finally managed to drag himself back into a seated position. He looked like a man who had been alone without food or water on a desert island for several months. His hair had fallen out, his rib cage showed clearly in his emaciated chest and his eyes were sunken. They burned red with rage and hatred and also fear.

"Is zis why you made me? Just to torture me?"

"I'm not trying to torture you. I just need to feed. As a Vampire, I'm sure you understand."

"Zen let me feed too," begged Yuri. "Master, please. Let me grow stronk on blood of veak so zat I kan serve you better."

"I need to contain this."

Yuri laughed weakly. "Ven vill you feed again?"

"Tomorrow. A little earlier, I think. So I'm not as desperate. Also, if I feed every day, I won't take as much each time."

"You'll take more each time," predicted Yuri.

That was true, so Vass said nothing.

"I von't recover by tomorrow even if you take the same amount," Yuri added.

Seeing the damage done to the Vampire, this also was likely true.

"Vat do you even take from me?" asked Yuri. His voice was raw and rough. "You don't drink blood like Vampire."

"You and I feed on the same thing," said Vass. "But because there's still an element of humanity left in you, you need blood as a conduit. I don't need any conduit. I can mainline it."

"But what is it?"

"It's your soul. I'm feeding directly on your soul."

Yuri shuddered.

"You agreed to this," Vass reminded him heartlessly.

The Vampire began to sob again, quietly. There was something truly horrible about watching a strong man cry.

"I vorked for you for fifteen years," Yuri said. "But I nothing to you, am I? I zought you had chosen me for great honor because I had proven myself to you. But anyone vould have vorked. You just needed piece of meat. You may call it soul, but it's niet different zan meat of dog for you. Soul—zis is supposed to be something precious and unique created by Light. But not to you."

"Do you think you're precious and unique?" sneered Vass. "Do you think the Light cares what happens to you?"

"No," rasped Yuri. "I vorth nothing."

Vass wasn't even certain he said those last words out loud, or if they only came as a whisper from inside his mind. Yuri collapsed into a tight ball, clinging to his knees, and hiding his face. It was the same position that Naya had taken when he had broken her soul. And now Vass saw it happen again, this time with Yuri.

Right there in front of Vass, the man's soul shattered and broke. The light died in his aura, and he was surrounded by a cloud of black despair.

Vass tried to back away as if some threat had entered the room. He backed up all the way to the cement wall, hitting his head against the low ceiling. He cursed, rushing up the rest of the rickety wooden steps to ground level. He stood outside, under a spangled August sky. He stared up at the stars, but they were cold and far away and did not speak to him.

Eighteen

August 18, Thursday
(New Day)

WHATEVER WEIRD MOOD had overtaken Vass on Wednesday, by Thursday morning he seemed completely recovered. He went back to work as if nothing had happened. As usual, Naya had work to do, including those tasks she had to catch up on because she had taken time to do her pottery. She still had to fire both pots. She did not have a pottery kiln, so she would definitely have to go over to Sylvia's Pottery Yard if she wanted to do that. She procrastinated on the grounds that she had too much work right now. Maybe on the weekend.

By dinner time, Vass was acting weird again. Naya had gone shopping during the day while doing her rounds and purchased some extra ingredients for her own meals in case he wanted to share mushroom stew. But she sensed that although he ate his portion like a starving man, he didn't really relish vegan food. So, she relented and also bought some chicken and hamburgers. It wasn't steak, but she wasn't sure how to cook that anyway.

To her disappointment, he once again refused dinner and hid in his room. She wanted to respect his privacy, but when she heard things knocking around, she was too worried to stay out any longer. She opened the door.

The room was a mess. He had knocked the ceramic sink to the floor and shattered it. He had overturned the bed. He'd even punched a hole in the plaster wall, and if the bloody marks on the stones or any indication he had tried to punch those walls as well. Now he was curled up in a ball in the middle of the floor, shaking and sweating.

Unfortunately, Naya knew exactly what was wrong with him.

Riley and Bran, her two crew heads, both answered her call. She needed their muscles to help control Vass. While they literally tied him down in the bed, she swept up the broken things from the floor so that no one would step in it. Judging by the bloody cuts on his feet, she was too late for Vass.

"I told you that you should give drug tests to new employees," Bran said. The Bear Shifter hated drug addicts. Probably because his own brother was one, and he couldn't stand the reminder.

"A drug test wouldn't have picked this up," said Riley. "This guy is not addicted to anything from Mundania. It's much worse than that."

"Dark magic?" Naya asked. She knew some arcanes got addicted to dark magic the way humans became addicted to meth or cocaine. But she had tested Vass and not sensed any sign of dark magic.

She told that to Riley.

"I can't explain that," Riley admitted, "but if it's not dark magic, it's something even worse. Something that goes even deeper. Could even be a curse. I don't think it's just a physical problem, it seems to go all the way down to the spirit." He shook his head. "I don't know how to help you with this, Naya."

"I'm not the one who needs help."

"I definitely don't know how to help *him*. But I'm as concerned about him as much as I am about *you*. I know your mother-hen instinct is kicking in. But whatever is eating up this guy... I think it's beyond any of us."

"What would you have me do?" she asked. "Just drive him out of our territory past the shield and dump him there? Then lock him out?"

"You gave him a week's probation, and he couldn't even get through that. I'd say he hasn't learned anything from you."

"But he's been trying so hard."

"Sometimes that's not enough." Riley ran his hand through his hair. "You and I both know that, Naya."

"You got past it, Riley," she said. "Maybe not soon enough to save what we had, but you at least used our breakup as a wakeup call. What did you do? Whatever you did, why can't he do it too?"

"There's a group that meets in the basement of the church in town..." Riley said reluctantly. "I could take him there. It's for dark magic users, and I don't know if that's what his problem is. Like I said, it seems almost like a curse or something worse than an ordinary addiction. And he has to be willing to go. You know that."

"I'm going to sit with him tonight," she said. "And tomorrow, if that's what it takes. Through the weekend if he needs it."

The two men exchanged a long hard look. They knew her well enough to know there was no arguing when she got into 'healing nurse' mode.

"Then we're going to stay too," said Bran. "But if you really want us to go into the weekend, we might lose a day of work."

"You don't have to stay," said Riley. "I'll take a sick day. My crew can handle it without me for one day."

"So can mine," said Bran. "Anything Wolves can do, Bears can do better."

That started some playful teasing between the two of them, continuing the long-standing rivalry of Bears versus Wolves.

"You know, I just thought of something," said Bran. "It was advice given to my brother. He didn't take it, but that doesn't mean it was bad advice. If a Shifter is addicted to something, supposedly shifting to his other form can help lessen the withdrawal symptoms. Of course, that applies to things like alcohol and drugs. I don't know about dark magic."

"Shifting could make it worse," said Riley.

But Naya knew Riley hated shifting to his other form, so she wasn't certain she should accept his claim at face value.

"Has Vass shifted since he's been here?" she asked.

Both foremen shook their heads.

"I don't even know what he is," said Bran. "Except I know he's not a Bear. Or a Wolf."

"I have a suspicion, but I could be wrong," admitted Riley.

~

August 19, Friday Morning
(New Day)

Vass woke up feeling like hell—hungry, hungover, hating life.

For a moment he thought he had done Monday all over again and panicked. He was so damn sick of that day. Then he realized the light was all wrong and he was in Naya's guest room.

Also, the modder'f'king Werewolf was sitting next to him.

"What are you doing here?" Vass tried to sit up and discovered he was strapped down to the bed. "Soma'a'vitch!"

"Good afternoon to you too," Riley said sardonically.

"Why is it afternoon? What day is it? Why am I tied to the bed?"

"You tell me."

Vass glowered at him.

"You went into withdrawal, asshole," said the Werewolf. "Anybody else would've kicked you out on your ass, like you clearly deserve. But Naya has a soft spot for losers. She told us to dry you out. She sat with you all night herself and then dragged us in for the second and third shifts. We are doing this instead of real work. You're welcome."

As soon as Riley said in it, Vass felt the cravings crash over him like a tidal wave. And there was Riley, sitting there with his brightly burning soul, looking like a tasty meal in the spirit world. The idiot thought these silver chains would hold a demon because they would work on a Shifter. The idiot Werewolf had no idea how much danger he was in right now.

Don't feed on him, Vass told himself. *If you need to feed, go back and use the Vampire again. He's had two days of rest now.* But was that enough? Vass had taken too much last time. Yuri would not survive another feeding.

Riley would.

Werewolves were strong. As strong as Vampires. There was so much light in Riley's aura...

No! No feeding on Yuri. No feeding on Riley. No feeding on Naya. No feeding on anyone. He knew he felt like shit because the Infernal Machine was feeding on him. But he also knew that it wouldn't kill him. As a demon, he was the conduit the Infernal Machine needed to the rest of the living beings in the Spheres.

Vass remembered seeing demons who were punished by being cut off from any slaves. He'd never understood why they acted as though they were being tortured just because they didn't have slaves tending them anymore. Now Vass understood. It wasn't servants they wanted, it wasn't someone to pour their wine or warm their bed. The starving demons wanted to feed on the souls of their slaves, to prevent the Infernal Machine from feeding on them.

But those demons, although they screamed and begged for mercy, did not die from being starved of what they craved. In fact, you could torture a demon for centuries like that. The demon would get thinner and thinner, yet never die. The Infernal Machine would not give up a conduit to the thing the beast craved for itself. Souls. Precious unique souls.

I won't die no matter how much it hurts, Vass told himself. So I can endure this. I just have to be stronger than the craving.

"I know what you're thinking," Riley said.

"I doubt that very much," said the demon.

"You want to break the chain of the addiction. And you're thinking that you're strong enough to do this alone. But you're not."

"F'ck you."

"But you don't have to do it alone."

"No one's going to help me," said Vass.

"Look around you, dumb ass. We're helping you right now."

Nineteen

August 19, Friday Evening
(New Day)

"THIS IS THE PLACE," said Naya, pulling her pick up into the parking lot. She had offered to let him drive his own truck, but he still insisted it was a gift to her. Honestly, it would've been much harder to park the monster truck in the parking lot behind the church than her rusty old Chevy.

"Have you ever been here before?" he asked.

"Not me, but Riley went for a while. Besides, I know the pastor. Everyone does."

"He was a dark magic addict? Not the pastor. Riley."

"No, he was on something specific to wolves. But I think the principle of any addiction is the same."

Vass didn't argue with her, but Naya thought he looked dubious.

The meetings were held in the basement of the church. He didn't show any signs of going in by himself, so she took his hand and went with him. She would sit through the entire meeting with him if that's what he needed. She wasn't sure why it mattered to her. It was strange. She felt as if they had known each other for a year even though it had only been a few days. At night, she had dreams about him. Sometimes he was wonderful in the dreams, an exquisite lover, a man who tried to cook for her even though hilariously he cooked steak not realizing she was vegan. But other dreams morphed into nightmares. He turned cruel and mocking, he even assumed a terrible shape that was like a mixture of different animals.

When she woke up, she suspected the dreams reflected her uncertainty about what kind of shifter he was and her awareness that he had a kind heart but a dangerous addiction. Like anyone who was a slave to a substance, when he didn't get his fix, he could turn into a nasty devil. Just because it wasn't how he wanted to act when he was with her didn't mean that it was safe for her to be with him.

She knew all that, and yet here she was.

They entered the room before the meeting started. Naya didn't want to arrive late and allow Vass to use that as an excuse to turn around and not go in. On the other hand, arriving early had its problems too. It gave him time to give in to his doubts and turn around.

"Don't chicken out on me, okay?" she asked, appealing to his pride. He was a proud man, something she respected about him. In her opinion a man *should* take pride in his work and in building a good life for himself and the people who cared about. "I know this is scary to you, scarier than fighting an entire wolfpack, but you can do it."

"Thanks for the pep talk," he said sarcastically. "I was really trembling at the sight of those hideous folding chairs."

Despite his snarky attitude, he held her hand tightly, like a life raft.

The pastor had not arrived yet. The Dark Magic Users Anonymous consisted of about half men and half women. Naya did not know what kind of arcanes they were, although she could sense they all had magic.

"This is ridiculous," muttered Vass. "What the hell am I doing here?"

"Give it a chance," she urged him. "If you back out now, I'm not going to believe you left because you thought it was silly. I'm gonna believe you were a scaredy-cat."

"I know what you're doing," he said. "Do you think I don't recognize your pathetic manipulation techniques? Please. I'm a master at those."

She just smiled. "You're angry because you know I'm telling the truth."

～

Vass honestly didn't know anymore if he was doing this just to play along with what Naya wanted, part of his long con, or if he was really seeking help. Who was fooling whom at this point?

Maybe if there were some hope of breaking the Chains his father had put upon him, if there were some way to free himself from the Infernal Machine, he *would* seek help. Honestly and truly. He recognized now that he was as much a slave as any other denizen of Darkpyre. What difference did it make if he had a higher notch on the post if he had no real freedom? He was just another form of food to the Beast. The Beast didn't care about Vass, any more than Vass cared about Yuri. Even less. At least Vass had *tried* to stop feeding on his former employee. Like Vass, the Vampire would suffer terribly locked in his cage in the root cellar, yet he would not die.

That sounded so stupid. As if Yuri would thank him for the fine distinction of one form of torture over another.

Vass buried his head in his hands. Nothing was going to help. Nothing this stupid group that met in a basement talked about was going to help break chains that had been put on him by the Demon King of Darkpyre himself. His father was the master of all forms of addiction. Vass had no hope of overcoming power like that.

Finally, the clock struck nine and the pastor hurried down the stairs exactly on time. Without any expectation of seeing someone with magic strong enough to help him, Vass glanced at the leader of the Dark Magic Users Anonymous group therapy session.

"F'ck." Vass's face turned white. "I can't stay here."

Vass turned his head away from the pastor and hissed at Naya. "We have to go *now*."

"What's the problem?"

"I already have a history with this guy. He can't help me."

The man coming into the room was babbling to the group, apologizing for being late, even though he was not late.

Vass looked around for any other entrance to the room, but of course there was only one door down into the basement. He grabbed Naya by the hand and started edging around the room so he could avoid letting the newcomer see him as he departed.

They had made it all the way to the top of the basement steps when suddenly the pastor appeared out of thin air right in front of them.

Of course he did. Because he was an angel. A Seraph, to be precise. Not to mention the Guardian of the Fifth Path, the Hierophant. And if Vass had not been suffering from constant headaches, tremors, dry mouth, the urge to vomit and punch something, he would have remembered that "Pastor Mike" worked at this church as his human cover.

"Leaving so soon, Vassily Glug'ulgros?" the Seraph, 'Pastor Mike,' chirped. "You just got here."

"Hello, Michael." Vass smiled tightly.

"Chet is looking for you," Michael said. "He'll be very happy when I tell him that I've found you at last."

"No!" said Naya sharply. Both men had forgotten she was there. But she was there, gripping Vass by the arm and glaring at Michael as if *he* were the demon trying to steal Vass's soul and not the other way around.

"Look," said Naya. "Vass said you two have some history. I don't know what it is. Maybe he's come to you for help before and then relapsed. Maybe something worse." Her head darted back-and-forth between two men glaring at each other. "Okay," she sighed. "Obviously something worse."

"Well," said Michael. "He did try to kidnap me on more than one occasion."

"Kidnap you?"

"For my father," Vass explained blandly. "He wanted the good pastor to do some work for him and Michael refused. I was supposed to force Michael to do it. I didn't succeed."

"Not for lack of trying."

"That... Okay... that is much worse than I thought," admitted Naya. "But Vass didn't know you were going to be here, Pastor Mike."

"He knows where I work," Michael said.

"I honestly forgot." Vass's head felt like someone was hitting him with a hammer.

"He came here seeking help for an addiction," Naya insisted.

"You also told Chet you were interested in seeking help," Michael reminded him. "And then you threw him off a cliff."

~

"What?" gasped Naya. "You *murdered* someone?"

"The asshole obviously survived," snapped Vass. "Look, Michael, I made a stupid mistake coming here. I wasn't after you. Unless you wanna fight, just let's just walk away."

"You stole Chet's truck. There's going to be a fight, whether I want it or not," said Michael.

"Is that the truck you gave me as a gift?" Naya asked.

"Yes," Vass admitted. "What Michael forgot to tell you is that I only stole Chet's truck and threw him over the cliff because he was trying to kill me. You remember how I was the first time you healed me. Guess who did that? Chet."

"And he's going to do much worse when he catches up to you," warned Michael.

Naya frowned. "I don't even know who this 'Chet' guy is... "

"He runs the luxury automobile outlet," said Michael.

"Oh. The one on the local TV commercials? Who used to be a football star? He's quite handsome..."

"He also wants to kill me," growled Vass. "Wait, how do you even know about those commercials? I thought you didn't watch TV."

"I do have a TV which I keep in my closet, usually, but sometimes I watch the local magic channel... Never mind, we are getting off topic." She addressed to the pastor directly.

"All I know is that you're supposed to be a pastor, and you are supposed to be helping people overcome darkness and addiction in their lives. My friend needs help. We can return the truck. No one is even using it. I'm sure the only reason he didn't return it before was that he was afraid this other guy would try to kill him or have him arrested if he did."

She darted a glance at Vass. He was extremely tense, with his fists clenched at his side, but he was also still trembling from the symptoms of withdrawal. It was like Riley had said, whatever he suffered, it was closer to a curse than any other form of withdrawal she had seen. It has been days now and he was still suffering as badly as the first night. In fact, his symptoms seem to be getting worse rather than better.

"Naya," asked Michael, "How did you meet this... man?" There was a slight hesitation before he said the word *man* as if he was about to use a different word and changed his mind at the last minute.

"The usual way. He was hurt and alone in the woods. I healed him. Then it turns out he was able to fill a job opening I had, so he's been working for me since Monday."

"That long. I bet it felt like a lot longer to you, though, didn't it, Vass?"

That meant nothing to Naya, but to her surprise, Vass hung his head as if ashamed of something. There was a lot going on underneath the surface between these two men.

Just when she thought that the pastor would do something that triggered Vass to either fight or run, Michael visibly relented. His expression changed and he studied Vass with a very different expression. Pastor Mike murmured, "Seeing you two together, it just occurred to me... No, I must be dreaming... There's no way..." He was talking to himself now.

"Pastor Mike?" Naya asked.

Pastor Mike focused on her and then on Vass. "I want to give you a chance, Vass. As a counselor, I have a right to maintain the privacy of my patients. If you come into the meeting, I won't tell anyone you were here. Not Chet, not even you know who. None of the others."

"How many people has he pissed off?" Naya asked.

"A lot," said Vass.

"Are you really here for help?" Michael asked, searching his face, trying to meet his eyes. But Vass wouldn't lift his head. He stared at his feet as if suddenly fascinated by his shoes.

"I don't know," said Vass.

"At least that's an honest answer," said Michael. "Come back inside. Naya, maybe you should go home."

"I'll wait here," she said. "I have to drive him home." Sarcastically, she added, "He doesn't have a truck of his own, apparently."

Twenty

August 19, Friday Evening
(New Day)

WHILE SHE WAS WAITING for the session to end, Naya strolled around the edge of the parking lot, brushing the vegetative minds of the trees with her mind. None of them were sentient trees like her Hamadryad but she enjoyed their peaceful, liquid non-thoughts.

A shadowy man stepped out from the trees. Naya was startled. She was certain he hadn't been there before, which meant despite his shabby appearance and drawn face, he was a powerful magic user.

"Naya Fairchild," he said.

Given the circumstances, she might have felt frightened, but she didn't sense any threat from him. In fact, she realized she had met him before. He'd been the judge in a case her company had been involved in when some poachers had been attacking creatures on her land.

"Judge Renaci?" She asked. She might not have remembered him so well except she'd had the strangest dream about him recently, in which she'd found his body drained by a Vampire.

Raziel Renaci grimaced as if not entirely pleased she recognized him. "Retired. I wanted to warn you about Vass."

Naya stiffened. "What about him?"

"He's using you. He wants something from you."

"What does he want?"

"I can't tell you."

"I'm sorry but I can't take a warning like that seriously," Naya said. "Not without anything specific or concrete."

"I'm not permitted to say more."

"Are you a friend of Michael?"

Raziel Renaci looked sad. "I don't know how to answer that."

"You don't look well, Judge Renaci. You should come by my cottage and let me give you some healing Waters..."

He shook his head.

"Why not?" she asked. "I don't know what's been done to you, but I can sense something broken. If you are broken, seek healing."

"No."

"You came to warn me about Vass, but at least he is asking for help. You're rejecting it."

"Be careful, Naya. Don't give your trust to someone who can only destroy it."

He withdrew into the forest. Then he vanished.

∾

August 19, Friday Evening
(New Day)

The group meeting seemed utterly pointless to Vass, but he went through the motions. After the session, Michael asked him to stay after everyone else left. Vass wondered if Michael was going to go back on his pledge not to report him to the other Guardians. Surely Michael's loyalty to the Guardians and his duties as a Seraph and the Hierophant outweighed any responsibilities he had in his human capacity as a counselor.

"Is your father dead?" Michael asked.

That was the last question Vass expected. "No. Why would I be here if he were dead? I would be fighting my half-siblings and other sycophants for his throne back in Darkpyre."

"Then you admit you're still on their side? "

"I never denied that! What does it have to do with anything? Earth is supposed to be neutral territory."

"Except your side is scheming to invade this Sphere."

"What do you know about it?"

"We can't talk about things like that if we're on two different sides of a war, Vass. We can talk about you and your personal problems. That's it."

This was never going to work, Vass thought. Out loud, he asked, "Why did you ask if my father was dead?"

"I've never seen so many chains on any demon except a king," said Michael quietly.

"He was conferring a great honor on me," said Vass. In his mind, he remembered Yuri's bitter accusation, *I thought you had chosen me for a great honor... but you just needed a piece of meat...*

"Is that what he told you?" Michael asked. "You had to have accepted them willingly. Chains like this cannot be forced on anyone. Even now, you could remove them if you wanted to."

"You don't think I want to be free of these chains? Do you have any idea what they're doing to me right now?"

"I didn't say you could remove them alone. But if you asked for help…"

"I came here, didn't I?"

"I can give you something for the pain," said Michael. "It will help you manage the symptoms, but it won't solve the problem. You have to break the chains."

"Nothing can break them. They were forged in the Pit. I think you know which one I mean."

"Yes, I know."

Vass sank into his seat. "Then you know they can't be broken."

"They *can* be broken. You've already taken the first step by refusing to feed them. You know that the more you feed them, the stronger they grow, right?"

Vass stared. "No, I thought it was the other way around. They feel like they're getting stronger and stronger."

"I know it *feels* like that, but the opposite is true. It hurts more and more because they are getting weaker and more desperate. Like a cornered animal. They are alive, you know. Tentacles. That's what they look like in my vision. Like tentacles from some giant squid, sucking the life force out of you. But the longer you go without feeding them, the the slower they eat. They can't kill you. They are parasites. They die if you die."

"That much I know. But you're saying it's going to hurt me more and more, the more slowly they feed on me. F'cking fantastic. What if I can't take the pain anymore and start feeding just to end the agony?"

"You could come to the Castle for help."

"How would that help?"

"If you allowed us to lock you in the dungeon, with physical chains, enchanted to restrain you, you couldn't feed on someone no matter how much you had the urge."

Great, they wanted to do to him what he had done to Yuri. How appropriate.

"No way," said Vass "You all can go f'ck yourselves. I told you before I haven't changed sides. I just don't want to feed on anyone while I'm here on Earth. When I get back home, it will be a different matter. I can eat as many slaves as I want."

"If you weren't here to kidnap me, then who are you after?" asked Michael.

"I'm not after anyone."

"Bullshit," Michael said bluntly. "You're always after someone. Souls are your currency, your coke, and your food, all rolled into one. Is it Naya? Is she your target?"

"I'm not going to hurt the Dryad. Do you have something that can help me or not?"

"Actually, she is the one who has the medicine. Ask her to mix Waters from the Four Quarters. She will know what to do."

～

As Naya drove them both home, Vass related what Pastor Mike had told him. "Waters from the Four Quarters. He said that you would know what that meant."

"I do," she said. "But I don't know why he thinks I can do it."

"Maybe he was lying,"

"No," she said, "He wasn't lying. There is a simple magical formula for spiritual healing that involves making mixing equal portions of waters from the Spheres with different Elemental magics. The soothing waters restore balance and equipoise. The waters reduce the excess of any experience. It can be used for subduing manias, such as the dancing mania that broke out at the Leprechaun concert two months ago. But, usually, it is used to reduce pain rather than excess joy. I can make some. I have the correct waters and I know how to mix them. But I'm worried it won't be enough. What about a long-term solution? You don't seem to be coming out of withdrawal like people with other addictions I've seen. How long can you live like this?"

"Centuries. But I would prefer to drink your water."

"Vass..." Naya hesitated. "I don't know if I should tell you this. Someone in the parking lot warned me about you."

"Who?"

"I'm not sure it's right for me to violate his privacy."

"Then let me guess. Raziel Renaci."

She tilted her head, not quite acknowledging it. "His warning seemed urgent, yet vague. He said he wasn't 'permitted' to say more. Do you know what he was talking about?"

"Yes," said Vass.

But instead of sharing that information with her, he brooded.

"Who is he?" asked Naya. "I mean, I know he's Judge Renaci, but is he a friend of Michael's? Or Chet?"

"He's my brother," said Vass.

Twenty-One

August 26, Friday
(New Day)

ANOTHER WEEK PASSED in real time. Clean. Although it was only a fraction of the time he had spent on his do-over days using the Chariot of Heaven, Vass cherished every moment because he knew it was real, not only for himself but for those around him. At first, he found it humiliating that everyone on the crew knew about his problem. But gradually he realized that really meant everyone on the crew knew—and still accepted him.

On Friday in the third week of August, both crews in the yard team and Naya and her two friends Sylvia and Posey and some other girls that were either girlfriends or sisters of the guys who worked for Timber Falls met up together at a bar for beer, barbecue and karaoke. It was "August 80's Night" at The Woodland Grill, owned by Bambi Woodland. "Bambi" was Sylvia's grandfather: a gnarly, wooly haired old Faun who was grumpy, gruff, and beloved by everyone. The barbecue served huge racks of pork ribs and nacho-style fries, but they also had a side menu, and it included some vegetarian items for the Woodland fae. Naya was not the only dryad or nymph who was vegan. But most of the Shifters wanted meat, lots of it. Sylvia, although a Faun, fell in the meat camp.

After dinner they sang karaoke. There was a girl that Vass had never met until tonight who sang so beautifully that everyone in the whole bar fell silent, completely entranced. There was magic in her song. Nothing malicious, and nothing obvious. It was pure and subtle and filled with light. Vass wondered if she was a siren or even possibly a Seraph.

"Oh, that's Lyra," said Naya. "She's a demi-bird shifter—a Naangfa. I think her animal form is a wood thrush."

"Does she have any Water magic like you do?" he asked

"I don't know. As far as I know she doesn't have any magic except the ability to sing very beautifully. Some people say that Naangfa, whom the Greeks confused with the fish-tailed sirens, have the same ability as sirens, to so entice others with their music that they can lure them off cliffs or to become lost in the woods. But Lyra isn't luring any tourists to their deaths, don't worry. Why?"

"I just wondered if she had received a Calling." He chuckled. "Maybe not directly from a river goddess like you did."

"I never told you I had received a calling from a river goddess."

"I'm sure you did. When you told me you were interested in becoming Temperance."

"I never said I was interested in becoming Temperance. You knew it, yet I never told you. Just like I never told you I had received a calling from the River Spirit. Who told you that? That was private information. Was it Sylvia?"

"I don't remember," he said stiffly.

～

Naya frowned.

This wasn't the first time that Vass knew something he couldn't possibly know unless she had told him. Or unless one of her close friends had betrayed her confidence. Either way she couldn't make sense of it, and it bothered her. If it had happened just once, she would have blamed herself, but it happened over and over again. Naya wanted to pursue it, but right at that moment, her friends urged her to take a turn at the karaoke. Of course, nobody wanted to sing right after Lyra.

Finally, Naya allowed herself to be dragged to the stage, although she could hit about 3 notes on either side of middle C and that was as far as her range extended. It was August 80's Night so Naya chose a song originally by Cyndi Lauper, which the country music star Skyla Raye had recently re-popularized with a heartfelt cover. Naya's cover wasn't nearly as good, and she only knew half the words. She struggled with some of the verses:

Secrets, stolen, from deep inside—
   the drum beats out of time.

But she belted out the chorus with much more enthusiasm than skill:

If you're lost, you can look, and you will find me,
time after time.
If you fall, I will catch you, I will be waiting,
time after time.

She did her best, laughing along with everyone else as she slaughtered the high notes and struggled like a toad to hit the low notes. Everyone was hooting and clapping by the time she finished.

"I told you I couldn't do everything well," she chortled when she returned to sit next to Vass.

"You were the best one up there," he told her.

"Liar."

"You are the best one to me."

The way he said it, the hunger in his eyes which was all for her and nothing else, the heat that radiated from his body as he reached out to touch her—yet held his hand just a fraction of an inch away from her cheek—made her catch her breath.

Suddenly she felt another powerful wave of déjà vu. "We've never been here together before, have we? Did you ever come here before you met me? Maybe we were both here at the same time and I just didn't know you then..."

"This moment is totally unique," he said. "It has never happened before it will never happen again. No matter what happens, I'm here with you right now."

~

Outside, in the gravel parking lot behind the barbecue place, a spontaneous Shifter fight ring had formed.

"Oh no, not this again," said Naya.

Vass had been about to make the mistake of saying something similar. That would have given away the fact that he had already heard about this in previous versions of history during the Repeats.

"What is it?" he asked instead, as if mystified. Naya explained that the Shifters had a fight club, illegal by human standards. The biggest rule was that once a Shifter returned to human form, the fight ended. Fights to the death had to be allowed by the Alpha of each pack or clan of Shifters involved. All other fights were between the two men, or in some cases two women, who were fighting. About a quarter of the bouts were between women but it was not allowed for a male to fight a female. However, it was allowed for Shifters of different types to fight each other.

Tonight, the fighting had started with two females, Naya's friend Sylvia and Dezzie Boren, a Bear Shifter. Dezzie was a full animal shifter: she became a Bear during the full moon.

In one unfortunate iteration of his terrible Monday, Vass lost his temper, assumed his full demon form, and killed every single person in the lumberyard except for himself and Naya. She had fallen into the blood of her friends Bran and Riley, sobbing and cursing him. That had not been a good day. He was glad he had erased it.

The only thing he cherished about that day was the memory of her courage. He'd unleashed his full demonic wrath—and even then, she had still defied him. Her courage amazed him.

On other Repeats, Riley had challenged Vass to a fight, usually because Vass had mouthed off about something, and Vass had slain the Werewolf. Not everybody, just the one guy, but Naya had still been pretty bent out of shape about it. That's when Vass had been informed about the rules of Shifter fights and how he'd violated even blood Shifter norms. Thank the dark powers that Naya would never know how many truly bad days he had to go through to finally behave like a normal person around her.

A couple more fights passed, and he wondered if he should ask for another set of the calming Waters. He didn't want to lose his temper. However just glancing over at Naya had the same effect as the water itself. He felt centered and soothed. Despite the seeming violence of the fights, everyone was having a good time. This wasn't like gladiatorial pits back in Darkpyre, where the doomed were forced to fight to the death against their own loved ones so that they would emerge as losers whether they won or lost the game itself.

~

Riley was tagged by the winner of the last fight to be the next fighter. That was how it worked. The winner tagged the next Challenger, and the Challenger could tag anyone he liked from the circle to be his opponent.

"Who should I fight?" Riley asked the crowd.

"Bring it on," said Bran.

"If you weren't a boy, and too fragile for me," said Rowena, one of the Grayhide pack, "I would say the same."

"How about you, Vass?" Riley asked.

Vass narrowed his eyes. "That's a bad idea." (I could kill every one of you, you stupid f*ck wits.) "You would lose."

"Put your money where your mouth is."

"Riley," cautioned Naya.

"We both know he's a fighter, Naya. He has to fight sometime."

"He doesn't, actually. He doesn't have to fight anyone. You can actually live your entire lifetime without fighting anyone."

"You can, Peacemaker, but Vass is a Shifter. It's in his nature. Come on, Vassily. Show us your animal side. What do you think you're hiding? I already know what you really are."

"If you did, you wouldn't be challenging me."

"Maybe I would." Riley grinned. "Somebody has to drive Naya up to the Castle to audition for Temperance. She asked me to do it, but I'll let you fight me for the privilege."

"No way!" shouted Naya. "That's not fair. The only reason I didn't ask Vass is that he doesn't have a truck."

Vass knew that the real reason was that Naya knew he didn't want to drive into Arcana Glen, where he would probably encounter Chet. He had been just as glad because the last place he needed to go was the Castle. But now that Riley had thrown down the gauntlet, he knew he wouldn't refuse. Riley knew it too. Even Naya knew it and understood the primordial nature of the challenge could not be denied.

Vass stepped into the ring.

Twenty-Two

August 26, Friday
(New Day)

VASS COULD NOT BELIEVE how calm he was. The stench of indulgence and sin in the crowd, the screaming and shouting, the incitement to violence, and especially the hint of jealousy wafting off Riley should have been razzing him into a blood lust that he would not be able to control. That was usually how he felt when he had to get into brawls.

Instead, Vass felt a great quiet within him, like a pool in a forest. His body was buzzing with energy, but his mind felt still and undisturbed. He didn't hate Riley. His main concern in this fight was simply to not kill everyone. However, this ended, it wouldn't be with Naya sobbing over the bloody bodies of her friends.

He had faked many fights with Riley during the do-over days, where he had to take the fall in order to advance his agenda. In a way, he was doing the same thing now, except he didn't have any ulterior motive. He didn't need Naya to take him back to her cottage and tend his wounds so that he could trick her into signing her soul over to him. He just wanted this night to end on a high note for everyone.

"What is it you think you know about me?" he asked Riley.

"You're a Boar Shifter," said Riley. "And you have some beef with Wolves. That's what I would really like to find out. What happened? Did Wolves kill your parents?"

They were circling each other, but they were still in human form. Usually, these fights started out between two human men or women, but they always ended with two animals in the ring.

"You're pretty far off the mark," smirked Vass. "Your sense of smell led you astray. You sniffed swine on me, but I wasn't born a Shifter. I was born... Something else. A curse turned me into a pig."

Not long ago, as real time went, Vass would have slit his own throat before sharing this humiliating story with anyone. But whether it was during the do-over days or just in the last two weeks that he had been struggling with real pain from fighting the Chains' chokehold on him, he realized he no longer cared who knew the truth. If they thought less of him for it, f'ck'em.

However, no one in the crowd was laughing. They were hanging on every word of his story, especially Naya. She had heard a version of it before, but that time he had been shouting it as he sliced off people's arms and legs, and she had been screaming her head off, and anyway, she wouldn't remember that anyway, thank the Light.

"My father had the ability to uncurse me," continued Vass. "He is rich and powerful and has a lot of resources. But instead of helping me, he invited all of his friends to a big party, and he brought in some canine shifters, and he told them to hunt me for the entertainment of the guests. So, yeah, I don't like the smell of wolves. It's a visceral thing, nothing personal."

Riley was shocked. So were many of the people in the ring. "Holy shit, Vass... I had no idea...if you want to back out..."

"Some good did come of it," said Vass. "Not only did I finally find out who my real friends were, but ever since I had the curse lifted, I have found that I can shift anytime I want."

Vass shifted into a huge, tusked boar and attacked Riley.

～

Naya clasped her hands together and clenched her teeth. First, Vass shifted into a boar. Then Riley shifted into his wolfen form.

Two men she cared about were fighting each other and there were so many ways this could end badly. But Riley was right. Even though she was a peacemaker by nature, she was also part of the wild magic of the forest; she understood that violence was as much part of nature as peace. Even the trees, as gentle as they seemed to humans, were in constant competition with each other for sunlight.

And the trees often witnessed wild fights between the animals that lived within their branches and under their shade. She understood on some level that the two men were fighting over her. They were civilized enough that bloodshed would not decide who won her, and yet wild enough that they wanted to prove they could win her that way if they needed to.

She had never seen Vass fight in his animal form before. Nor did she know the story of what his father had done to him, although something about it triggered a sense of déjà vu. But Naya knew something else about Vass that Riley didn't. She had seen Vass fight a Vampire.

Maybe that was the reason she was more worried that Vass would lose control and kill Riley than she was about Vass losing the fight. Vass's only real fight was deep inside where no one else saw him struggling. But Naya saw.

The crowd knew how strong Riley was, and they were betting on him to win. They were shocked as hell when the fight ended with the boar ramming its tusk into the belly of the wolfen and tossing Riley so far across the circle that he slammed into Bran. The Bear Shifter staggered under the momentum.

Riley collapsed to the pavement. Vass galloped towards the fallen wolfen. At the last moment, Vass shifted back to human. He bent over Riley.

"Naya," said Vass. "He needs you."

She was already running to Riley's side. He shifted back into his human form. He was naked and covered in blood. However, as she felt his aura with her fingertips, she realized with relief that by some miracle none of his major organs had been punctured. The wound looked bad, but it was superficial. It was nothing that her magic could not handle. By the next morning, her healing potions, combined with Riley's inherent shifter healing strength would have him as good as new by morning. The hangover he would suffer from how much he had to drink tonight would last longer than the injury.

"Nothing was punctured," she announced for the benefit of the crowd.

"Thank goodness you have terrible aim with those tusks," joked Bran.

Vass smirked. "I have excellent aim."

But then the cocky expression changed into something more vulnerable. For a moment he looked like a little boy, looking at her for approval. She had absolutely no doubt that he had hit exactly what he aimed for. He had deliberately issued a blow that would end the fight without harming Riley too much. His expression asked her, *Naya, did I do good?*

She inclined her head. He smiled back at her with such happiness that her heart melted.

～

August 27, Saturday, Dawn
(New Day)

Sunrise over the lake made the water sparkle like gold. The liquid light shimmered, a mirror of the beauty of the luminous sky. The whole world was like an ewer pouring out light.

"Remember when I came up with this plan?" asked Vass.

"Seems like months ago, but I believe it was two weeks," said Raziel sardonically. He fiddled with a fishing rod. "We should invite the Ice Giant to go fishing. Does John fish? He seems like a guy that likes fishing."

"And you said there was an alternative," said Vass.

Raziel put down the fishing rod, suddenly paying attention. "Trade information on the Dark Triad for immunity from the Guardians."

"Yeah... I'm not ready to do that," said Vass. "But I need to get clean. I'm afraid I might relapse. I know I will. But I can't if they have me in the dungeon of the Castle."

"Are you serious?" gawped Raziel.

"I'm taking Naya to the Castle tomorrow."

"The Guardians will arrest you!"

"Especially since I'll arrive in Chet's truck."

"You're returning the Chariot to the Guardians? Is this some clever plan to use the Chariot again? To defeat the Guardians? To win Naya?"

"I think Naya is a Guardian. As soon as she realizes that, she'll find out who—what—I really am. Hopefully, she'll never know what I've done. Either way, I know I can't have her. But I have to do this." After a pause, Vass said, "Go ahead and laugh. After all those times I mocked you for betraying your side for a woman, look at me."

"There's a big difference. Naya is not..." Raziel trailed off.

"The woman who betrayed you? But you still won't tell me *her* name."

"Are you defecting, Vassily, or simply trying to trick your enemies into helping you get sober? I'm a little confused," Raziel said.

"Do you want to come with me?"

"To the Castle?" Raziel swallowed hard. "Do I have a choice?"

"Actually..." Vass yanked the black feather out of the ether. "Yes."

He thrust the feather at Raziel, who backed up a step. The boat rocked. Raziel had gone ashen. He looked bewildered, almost angry.

"What game are you playing, Vass?"

"I'm giving you your freedom."

"Why?" whispered Raziel.

"Last week, after I met with Michael, Naya asked me who you were. I told her you were my brother. Because you are the first person in my life who showed me what a brother is supposed to be. You feel so guilty about betraying your people that you think you don't even deserve to heal your injuries, but what you don't see is that just you being you, a decent person, you helped me realize... hey, that's what I want. You may think your halo is gone, but compared to the assholes in my life, you gave me a light to follow.

"You saved my life, Raz. But you also saved my soul.

"I have the key to your chain. Not my own. But at least one of us can be free."

Raziel took the black feather. But although he looked shaken, he didn't look as happy as Vass had hoped he would.

"I'm going to ruin your gift," said Raziel, "I'm going to disappoint you. Because I can't face them. I can't go back."

"Then at least stay free," said Vass.

～

August 27, Saturday
New Moon

On Saturday morning, Naya found Vass waiting for her at the door of the monster truck.

"You don't have to drive me to the Castle," Naya said. "I can take my own truck."

"We might as well return the Chariot at the same time that I drop you off. Don't worry about getting home. Once you're Temperance, you will probably get your own limousine."

"I doubt very much that I'm going to be chosen. Aren't you afraid to go to the Castle?"

"Why would you think that?"

"Something Michael said," she replied. Yet there was more to her hunch than that. Honestly, it was like something she had heard in a dream. She couldn't put her finger on it. She shrugged. "Am I driving or you?"

"You better drive. Just don't push the button with the hourglass on it."

"What does that do?"

"You don't wanna know."

Twenty-Three

There was something he wasn't telling her. And it wasn't just how awesome it was to drive the Monster Truck, although it was a superb machine that drove as smoothly as water flowed down a river.

Neither of them spoke on the drive down to Arcana Glen and then back up the hill to the Castle. Naya had a map which told her which driveway to take; it led around to the back of the Castle, where she was supposed to park. All of the Guardians who had been chosen so far, seven men and seven women, were waiting in a beautiful garden. It was a lovely summer morning, and the ladies were in sundresses and the gentlemen in casual clothes. It was hard to believe these were the dozen most powerful wizards and sorceresses in the Seven Spheres.

"That's strange," Naya said. "Pastor Mike is here."

Vass looked at her sidelong. "He is the Hierophant."

"What! Pastor Mike? But he's just... He's just *Pastor Mike*. Pastor Mike from the church on the street corner..." Another thought filtered through her shock. "And you knew this! You knew this all along, didn't you?"

He nodded curtly.

"What else aren't you telling me? Who are you really, Vassily? You're not a born Shifter. But you were already arcane even before you were cursed, weren't you?"

"I'm sure they'll tell you everything soon enough," he said wearily. "Whatever they tell you..." He trailed off. "It's all true. But what I'm going to tell you right now is also true. I..."

He paused. And then he kept trying to say something but didn't.

"Dammit, I don't know how to say it," he muttered finally. "Don't forget your pots. They're in the back."

"I know," she said. "I'm the one who put them there." They were ewers, not pots. And they were firmly packed in real feathers inside wooden boxes that she had packed herself.

Naya parked the Monster Truck near the garden. There were no other vehicles nearby. This would be a very intimidating interview, with just her and fourteen Guardians. She had hoped that Vass would stay with her, but she had an uneasy feeling, as if something terrible were about to happen.

As soon as they both climbed out of the car, several of the Guardians surrounded Vass, like cops around a criminal. They handcuffed his hands behind his back with something silver and wicked looking. They escorted him into the Castle before Naya could even finish her cry of confusion and dismay.

"Chet and Troy, Pastor Mike and Victoria the Dragon Empress, those I know already," said Vass to the bunch who cuffed him and hustled him into the cool subterranean hallways of the lower levels of the Castle. "Who is the cute little kitten?"

The diminutive Neko girl, who displayed kitty cat ears even in her human form, placed her hands on her hips. It only made her look more adorable. "That's the Guardian of Strength to you, bozo."

"Oh, you're the acrobat whose brother turns into a lion the size of Texas."

"What do you know of my brother?" she demanded.

"Only the same as you," he said, "That the lion escaped and everyone is looking for him, our side as well as yours. I don't know why they're so desperate. There are certainly enough dumbass Shifters in this damn town. You'd think they could just find another lion."

She hissed at him.

"Take the demon to the dungeon," said the Magician, striding toward the small clump of people with Vass at the center.

"I didn't have to come here, you know," Vass pointed out. He jerked his chin at Chet. "I returned his fancy car. And I brought you another Guardian. You should thank me."

"She can't claim her legacy alone," said the Neko girl. "You should've brought her boyfriend too."

"He wanted to come, but I didn't think Chet here would appreciate anyone else driving his Chariot. The boy shouldn't be hard to find. His name is Riley. He's a demi-shifter from Autumndelle, so he should make a good Pan."

Chet shoved his hands against Vass's chest, forcing Vass to step backward. The other demon, his former friend and recent enemy, glared at Vass. "Why did you really come here, Vass?"

"Michael suggested it. We've been hanging out quite a lot these last couple of weeks."

Pastor Mike was standing nearby, and all the warriors looked at him.

"Is that true?" asked the Magician.

Michael nodded.

"Why wouldn't you tell us?" demanded Chet. "You knew I was looking for him!"

"He came to me for help, and I told him he could get help here."

"You mislead him," said the Magician coldly. "The only thing he's going to get here is a dungeon cell."

"That's what I told him," said Michael.

Five of the Guardians, including Pastor Mike, the only one she knew, took Vass away from her. Nine remained. They dressed like normal people. The only one who gave a hint of her real power was the dark-haired woman who wore a hat with a veil. It could have been nothing more than a modish summer hat, but Naya suspected the woman used the veil as an anchor for a veiling spell to guard her mind from the constant barrage of other people's thoughts and emotions. If that was true, Naya knew who she was: the only one so sensitive that she needed to constantly veil her mind was the Seeress.

A little white puppy yapped around the feet of a golden-haired girl in a sunflower sundress, who swooped up the dog into her arms. At first, Naya thought the girl was in fact a teenager, but gradually Naya realized the young woman was older than she behaved. Naya's healing sense picked up the oddest sensation that the slender young woman was... pregnant? If so, she wasn't showing. Unexpectedly, the silly girl was the one who took charge.

"Hello, why don't you have a seat? Or would you like some help bringing your jars out of the truck? You do have jars or jugs or something, don't you? All the other men and women who came to talk to us about becoming Temperance did. The others each brought two boxes, but I see that you have four. Is it a guessing game or do you hope to win the position by being twice as watery?"

She talked as fast as a brook babbled. Naya wanted to scoop her up and place her in a quiet pool to calm down.

"Bethany, you haven't introduced yourself," chided the Seeress. She lifted her veil, to reveal huge violet eyes and pale, delicate features. "Or any of us."

"Oh, I'm sorry, my bad. Victoria is so much better at the proper forms. I'm Bethany, this is Kyrah, this is Maverick—he's a robot, it's so cool..."

One of the men stepped forward. "I'll take over and do the introductions, if you don't mind, *Sarmati* Bethany," he said. His words were respectful, but he winked at the blonde as if sharing an inside joke. "We all know how distracted you get."

"Why bother with introductions until we know if it's worth wasting time on her?" demanded the one Bethany had called Maverick and announced was a robot. He was certainly as cold as a machine, Naya thought, a little repulsed. And not very nice.

"I'm Owen, the Guardian of Fortune," said the man who took over. "This is Kyrah the Seeress. She is the one who will watch you perform your magic. After that... if it's warranted, I will introduce everyone else. Otherwise, we'll simply have to wipe your memory, because currently some of our identities are secret." The way his eyes twinkled, it wasn't clear if he was joking or not. "And we already know that you are Naya Fairchild."

"I understand," said Naya. "And to answer Bethany's question, I have only two forms of magic, Elemental Water and Elemental Earth. I have four ewers with me because I am also using them to summon magical Waters from the Four Quarters."

"What does that mean?" asked Bethany.

"It's an archaic term for the Elven Spheres," replied Owen. "Springvale, Summerland, Autumndelle and Winterdom. But, Ms Fairchild, you were not supposed to use the vessels prior to coming to us for the test. That is a requirement to prove there was no interference or outside assistance in the magic."

"I..." Naya had forgotten all about that. "I'm sorry," she said humbly. "I had to use them to help a friend. If it invalidates the test, I understand, and I won't waste any more of your time."

She started to walk back toward the parking lot and then recalled that she had arrived in a Monster Truck that did not belong to her.

"I... uh...I'm so sorry, I need to call a ride..." But, wait, she couldn't leave without Vass! Yet, somehow, Naya doubted the Guardians were going to let him leave with her. "Can you please tell me what is happening to my friend? Is he... under arrest?"

"He's a demon," said Owen. "Did you know that?"

"No, but I don't care," Naya snapped. However, after a moment, as his words sank in, she found herself reviewing many puzzling conversations and events. "Yes, I can see how that fits with what he told me."

And that was what he was afraid to tell me, she added to herself. By the Light, he really could have killed Riley in that fight!

The Seeress gazed at her sadly. She had heard Naya's thought and responded with the whisper that touched Naya's mind gently. *We fear he deceived you because he was using you.*

"I'm not prejudiced against demons as such," claimed Owen. "Some of my best friends are demons. But Vass is also guilty of attempted kidnapping, attempted murder, and grand theft auto."

"But at least he returned the truck," Naya pointed out.

"You have one brown eye and one green eye!" exclaimed Bethany. "Did you know that?"

"Uh... yes, *that* I knew."

"She's not the one," Maverick said impatiently. "Why are we still talking to her?"

"I'll call you a taxi," said Owen.

Bethany stomped her foot. "No! We haven't seen her watery things yet!"

"Bethany," said Owen, rolling his eyes, "Pay attention. The test is invalid because she already used the pots."

"They aren't pots. They are ewers," Naya corrected automatically.

"Will you show us how you use the ewers to make the four flavors of water? That sounds pretty neat."

"If I do so, may I leave some for my friend? For Vass."

"The demon," said Owen.

"It's medicinal," explained Naya. She thought about explaining how much Vass would suffer if he didn't have the soothing waters, but she feared these people hated him so much they might see his suffering as a benefit. "Please."

"Bethany wants to see the medicine," said Kyrah. "Owen?"

"Fine," he grumbled. "Maverick, you're strong. Bring the boxes."

The other Guardians had remained seated in a semi-circle of fine lawn chairs. A few of them had been quietly talking amongst themselves. However, as Naya set up her ewers on a white garden table, the onlookers fell into a respectful hush. One of the men whose name Naya didn't know asked to inspect the ewers. He lifted every ewer upside down to demonstrate nothing fell out. The robot, Maverick, also examined them.

"I don't detect any technology other than kiln-fired ceramics," said Maverick. "Miles?"

"They look empty to me," said Miles with a shrug.

Naya sought calm inside herself. She ignored the people watching her and extended her awareness deep into the earth, through the wind up into the sky, into the heat that burned at the heart of all life and the water that streamed in the blood and the rivers that were the blood of the earth. Having come full circle, she next touched the mind of her hamadryad familiar, Quigley Quiverbark.

Quigley, are you there?

I am here, Naya. Are you at the Castle already? How time flies! I will help you.

She extended her mind to the River Goddess, the Elemental Spirit.

River Mother, are you there?

I am here. You have fulfilled your promise to me. It took you long enough. I will help you.

Naya opened the first ewer to Springvale. The waters of Springvale bubbled up inside. She poured the waters of Springvale out of one ewer into another. When that one was filled, she switched the ewers and poured the waters of Autumndelle into the first ewer. The nature of her magic juggled time and space so that the pouring pitcher was always full and the receiving vessel always had more room.

Bethany's jaw dropped. "Wow! No one else did that! Did you actually open a portal to another Sphere...*just to pour water?*"

Naya didn't reply. The next part was more difficult. She had to call on waters from lands whose Elements were not native to her magic. Nor did she have friends and familiars of the Wind and Fire.

Highest power, fountain of Light, connect me to the Spirit friends I need, she pleaded. Help me help one who needs me.

She felt a hot, fiery spirt touch her mind. *I will help you.*

She felt a cold, icy wind blow across her mind. *I will help you.*

With the help of friends from the other Spheres, and the highest power for good over seeing all, Naya repeated the pouring of the ewers with waters from Summerland and Winterdom.

"May I have a bottle with a top?" she asked.

Someone handed her a glass bottle with a cork. She poured equal amounts of all the four unique waters into the bottle.

"Please give this to Vass," she asked. "It will help him remain centered and calm."

Bethany took the bottle. "I'll do it!" She beamed at Naya. "Thanks!"

She skipped away with the bottle.

"I'll call you a ride to take you home," said Owen. "We'll consider your audition and let you know if you are the next Guardian of Temperance. If you don't hear from us, consider it a NO."

The five Guardians who had disappeared into the Castle reemerged. Naya was surprised to see that in addition to Pastor Mike, she recognized one of the men as a dragon-burn victim she had once treated; the woman with him had come looking for him.

The tall, slender, severe man whom she took to be the Magician pointed at her. "She can't leave yet. I have something to show her."

Twenty-Four

August 27, Saturday
New Moon

NAYA WONDERED if she would be arrested and thrown in a dungeon too. Perhaps for aiding and abetting a demon felon? Vass had never committed a crime in front of her, and she would say so. The Magician marched in front of her; Kyrah walked behind her. None of the other Guardians came. Bethany had disappeared, evidently to the Magician's annoyance.

"Where did she go?" the Magician asked.

Kyrah glanced at Naya. "She wanted to take a bottle of water to the prisoner."

The Magician sighed. "Don't even bother trying to explain that."

They brought Naya into a round room in the tower edged with glass curiosity shelves. A large bank vault sat opposite the door.

"Normally, we use this door to access the Temple of the Guardians," said the Magician. "But I'm going to open a portal to the Third Sphere."

"But that's not..." *possible*, Naya was about to say. Then she remembered who she was talking to. There were Seven Mortal Spheres, realms of existence accessible to different forms of magic; there were an additional Three Immortal Spheres that were accessible only to spirits released from physical form—and to the most powerful of all magic users. Magic from the Three Immortal Spheres included the power to alter Time and Space as well as the ability to summon the Dead back to life. Those weren't powers Naya ever wanted to mess with, but the Magician operated on a different level.

"The 'Monster Truck' that the demon stole was not a simple truck," said the Magician. "It was a *Merkavah*—a Chariot of Heaven. The demon prince Vassily Glug'ulgros used this to manipulate time to repeat his first day with you over and over again. My colleague, the Charioteer, to whom the Chariot properly belongs, tells me that Vassily accessed this power 371 days in a row. He lived an entire year with you, while you experienced only one day. After that, apparently, the demon let normal time resume, which he has been living at the same pace as the rest of us for the last two weeks."

"I had no idea," Naya said. She felt numb.

"Obviously." His lip curled.

Naya felt *stupid*. Stupid and *used* and... how could Vass have *lied* to her to this degree? How could he have concealed *an entire year* from her? Stealing memories from her that she had no chance to share, gleaning information from her day by day... No wonder he knew things he shouldn't, *couldn't* have known, no wonder he knew just how to smile at her, just what to say to her...

He's been manipulating me this whole time. I was so naïve—I had no clue. I thought he was a Boar Shifter for Light's sake!

Kyrah touched Naya's hand, the barest brush. A soft voice in her head: *The demon wanted something specific from you, Naya. We need to know what.*

"We need to see the days he erased from ordinary Time," said the Magician. "For the rest of the Seven Spheres, those days are gone, just as if they never existed. Only Vassily Glug'ulgros remembers what happened. But in the Immortal Sphere of Memoria, every version of every day, even those re-written by fate, are kept preserved. I can take you to the Sphere of Memory. But you are the only one who can relive the days. We can only see those days through you."

Kyrah spoke aloud, although her voice was soft. "It may be very, very painful for you Naya. At this point, you can't re-write your choices from then with what you know now; you can only re-live what you experienced then. But a part of you will stand outside your own memory with the knowledge you have now." Privately, Kyrah added, *If he spent that entire year raping you or torturing you, you would experience that again, with no way to change it.*

"I can pull you out at any time," said the Magician. "If events are too gruesome to bear. But the more you can endure, the more we will learn about his true intentions."

The whole ordeal horrified her. But she tried to be brave.

"How long will it take?" Naya asked.

"You will experience a year of the same day over and over," explained the Magician, "But the actual time that will pass will be only as long as it takes us to walk through a door, blink, and walk out again. Two or three minutes."

"But...for me... a year will pass."

"It will feel that way, yes."

"A year of torture..."

"Whatever he did."

We will be with you, Kyrah promised. You will experience it and yet stand outside the memory at the same time.

Gulping hard, Naya said, "Let us do it before I think too much about it and cannot go through with it."

∼

She stepped into Monday, August 15, two weeks ago. She watched Vass make an ass of himself, culminating in a fiasco in which he somehow managed to blow up the dry kiln, burn down half the lumber yard, and almost start a forest fire.

Then she stepped into Monday, August 15, two weeks ago. But one day forward for Vass. His second try.

His third.

His fourth.

And on.

And on.

And on.

To the last day before the first day Naya actually remembered, the last time he had used the Chariot of Heaven to reset time. When he seduced her, played on her sympathies with a lie about having a sister to trick her into signing over the deed to her property and then watched the news report on a Vampire—which she now knew he himself had created—which massacred school children.

~

Naya stared at the man in her bed as if seeing him clearly for the first time that day. In fact, she was. Her genuine sorrow over the deaths head dispersed every last bit of magic he had released into the room.

She glanced down at the papers she had signed and then at her own naked body. Suddenly she scrambled from the bed.

"You're not a Shifter, are you?" she accused him. "You're a demon. You... Every single thing you told me was a lie. You tricked me."

For some reason, her outrage at this hour infuriated him. He switched to his demonic form, which was bloated and hideous.

"That's right, and you had it coming because you made it so damn easy!" he belittled her. "You deserved it! You thought you were being so caring and compassionate but all you cared about was proving yourself to be a righteous person. Thanks to your mindless lust and your desperate virtue signaling, I got everything I wanted. But at least you were a good lay."

Standing in her bedroom, aware of the Magician and the Seeress witnessing how Vass had seduced and betrayed her former self, Naya burned with humiliation and rage.

She watched her former self melt into a puddle of self-loathing. She could feel it happening as if it were happening to her now, and yet another part of her stood aside, hating Vass instead of herself.

"So that's what he wanted then," said the Magician.

"Her soul?" asked Kyrah.

"The deed to her property. Her soul was just a bonus, from the demon's point of view."

Naya shuddered. *Just a bonus.*

~

Three minutes / a year later, the three of them stepped back out of the Immortal Sphere of Memory and back to Earth. Naya felt so exhausted she wanted to collapse into a heap, the way her Memory-Self had done.

"Your body is not really tired, but your mind is," explained the Magician.

"I want to see him one last time," said Naya. "I want him to know that I know. I want to throw it in his face that I took back the time he stole from me!"

Is that wise? asked Kyrah.

"He is powerless to harm her now," said the Magician. "Let her confront her demon."

~

The Magician and the Seeress did not escort her down to the dungeon. Instead, a housekeeper in a long garnet colored gown, almost Victorian in style, showed Naya to the bowels of the Castle.

Vass was sitting in a cell that had been luxuriously furnished with carpets, couches, a bookshelf and reading chair, a lamp, and a table beside a four-poster bed with velvet hangings. Iron bars walled him in on three sides. The last wall was rock. He sat in the reading chair, but he wasn't reading. He had his elbows on his knees, his head in his hands.

He looked up and blinked hopefully when he saw Naya. Whatever he read in her face shut down that hope.

"Naya? What's wrong?"

"What's wrong?" she spat. "What's wrong is that I saw what you did to me. I saw the days you lived without me. EVERY. SINGLE. ONE. It was a year of days, Vass! I got to see what you *really* wanted from me!"

The blood drained from his face. "But... how... I erased those... I never wanted you to have to live through that for real..."

"Well, guess what, I did, and I have!"

He shifted into his full demonic form and threw himself up against the bars so hard and fast that the cage rattled—his pig snout and arm thrust through the bars, weird stubby claws extended—trying to grab her. Naya jerked backwards.

"Is this what you wanted to see?" Vass demanded. His voice in this body was deep and raspy and distorted by his boar tusks yet magnified to a shriek. "This is what I hid from you. You blame me for that? Then, go ahead—look at me! See me as I really am!"

She stared at him. Then she turned and left the dungeon.

~

The Magician met up with Naya just outside the stair that led to the lower levels.

"I was looking for a way out," she said. Exhaustion had caught up with her again.

"You may rest here before you go home," the Magician said.

"No...please..." begged Naya. "I just want to go home to my Tree."

The Magician held out his hand to her. Naya was confused, since this was the first sign of physical interaction, or any friendly gesture, he had made toward her. She placed her fingers across his palm.

Immediately, the scenery around her flashed, lights blinded her, darkness swept over her, and then she stood in the woods on her own mountain, next to her own tree, Quigley.

The Magician nodded gravely and disappeared again without saying goodbye.

Naya sank to her knees amidst Quigley's gnarly roots, hugging his trunk as she wept. *Oh Quigley, Quigley, at least you are steady and true. Did you see what I saw? It's terrible and confusing. I lived a year in three minutes.*

Now you know how I feel, hummed the Hamadryad. His deep, rich thought-voice did not hold the same turmoil that Naya felt. *You experience life so fast and change so much, it's hard for me to keep up sometimes.*

*But that's not...*She started to say that wasn't what happened, but touching Quigley's deep, slow, green mind, she felt her own tumult slow down. Her thinking changed from whitewater emotions that overwhelmed her to deep, strong currents and finally to a calm, clear pool. At last, she could reflect on what she had experienced.

Vass did change, didn't he... Some of the changes were obvious: his mastery over the dry kiln, for instance. But other changes he'd undergone were subtle. At first, she'd not noticed because some of the worst things he did to her came near the start and near the end of his year, with a sort of strange lull in between. At first, he'd only been groping blindly to figure out how to behave, and the day he'd slaughtered all her friends was terrible; then, about a third of the way through the year, he started to improve; but at the "end," after he'd learned how to manipulate her, he reverted to his worst self. He'd seduced her, he'd called her names, he'd gotten children slaughtered and of course, he'd done what he had come to do, he'd forced her to sign over her deed and her soul to him.

But then he erased that day too—the day he got everything he wanted. Why?

Now that she had evened the playing field, she'd learned as much about him as he had learned about her. She knew why he hated his father. She knew that his best and only friend in the world was a Fallen Angel he pretended to dislike. She knew he hated mushroom stew but had eaten it over and over again, every day for much of a year, just to please her. And not every one of those days had ended with him getting what he wanted from her, whether in bed or in business, so why had he done it?

If every moment of every fake day he spent with her was just a game to him, why had he erased the day he *won?*

Twenty-Five

August 27, Saturday
New Moon

AS SOON AS SHE LEFT, Vass deflated back into his human form. He wanted to be alone, but the fiends had realized the best way to torture him was to continuously parade people through his cell to witness his humiliation. He'd started shaking already, but he had no more of Naya's water. Given the way she had looked at him, he wasn't likely to get more. He planned to crawl onto the four-poster bed, pull the curtains, and curl up in the fetal position when the waves of pain started to hit.

A small white bit of fluff yapped at him. It was some kind of small dog. Chasing the dog, a young woman entered the dungeon cell. She had loose blonde hair, wore a flouncy, happy dress covered with sunflowers and altogether looked as if she had stumbled into the dungeon from a children's picture book.

"Are you lost, little girl?" Vass asked sarcastically.

"Hullo, Vass, don't you remember me?" she asked. "Last time I saw you, we fought zombies together! Good times, am I right?"

"Bethany Dilly," he said. The Fool.

"Bethany Guiscard, these days," she corrected. The Fool—and the wife of the Magician.

"I brought you a present," said Bethany. She waved what looked like a glass soda bottle in the air. "I wondered why I was carrying this bottle around, and then I remembered it was for you."

"Go away, Fool," he growled.

"I think you might be a Guardian," she said.

Vass stared at her. "Your levels of idiocy truly reach titanic proportions."

"Alephander thinks so too," she added. She grinned. "It's kinda obvious, actually."

"Not to me."

"Nope, somehow it never is obvious to the ones closest to it. I never saw it coming either!"

"You never see anything coming."

"I saw this. I saw you. Not like Kyrah sees the future—but in my own way. As a dream. As a possible Thing that could happen, a thing that would be cool. Okay, I admit, for a long time, I thought Raziel was going to be Temperance. You'd be you, and he'd be your opposite.... It makes sense because Temperance is usually an Angel and Pan is usually a Daemon, and you love each other..."

Vass growled at her.

"...But not romantically, as it turns out. Too bad, I think it would have been fun. Naya is great, though. But what did you do to Raziel? Mercy helped him escape Darkpyre. Did you force him back, Vass?"

"No. He's probably at my mansion, eating my food. Also, there's a Vampire in my root cellar. You should probably do something about that."

"Awesome! I kept asking Alephander when I'd get to meet a Vampire, and now I will."

Vass contemplated how many ways the Magician would hurt him if Vass got his wife eaten by a hungry Vampire. "You should probably send Chet to get the Vampire."

Chet wasn't likely to get eaten, but Vass could hope.

"We can't really make you a Guardian until you switch to our side." Bethany blew air in and out of her cheeks. "Alephander is pretty adamant about that."

"I can't do that."

"Chet did it."

"Chet was the outcaste son of a pit slave. No one cared what he did. I'm the son of the King of Gluttony—the current reigning High King of Darkpyre."

"Ooooo, you're so special," she sing-song mocked him. "C'mon. You could switch if you wanted to."

"I'm literally chained to the Infernal Machine. Do you have any idea what that means?"

"Zero. Zilch. Nada."

"It's a huge honor, an amazing privilege, and gives me tremendous power. It's also the worst curse and the worst addiction and the worst form of slavery all rolled into one."

"A curse?" She stepped closer to the cage. "I can break curses."

"That's right. Raziel had me brush up against you to break the pig transformation spell I was under."

"Was that cute piggy really you?"

"I was not a 'cute piggy.' I was an immense and frightening boar."

"Maybe I can break your chains," said Bethany. She held one hand out, close to the bars. "Touch me."

Vass stepped backwards.

"Um, I'm over here, not back there. You do *want* this curse broken, don't you? You just told me it was the most terrible thing ever."

"Yes... but... did you miss the part where I mentioned it also gives me immense power? I have power equal to that of a demon king! And I need that power to finish... an important project. And the chains were put on me by my own father, to show me his trust in me."

Bethany brushed some hair out of her eyes. "I think you're a little confused, Vass."

"It won't work anyway."

She held her hand out again. "Try it. Last chance before I leave."

Vass stepped closer to her and slowly extended his hand. The shakes had started; his hand shivered and quaked uncontrollably as he reached for her. He touched her hand. He studied the spirit outline of the manacles and the chains. Nothing changed when Bethany touched him. He yanked his hand away.

"I told you it wouldn't work. You may be able to nullify curses, but you can't undo damnation."

"I guess not. Sorry." Bethany dropped her hand sadly. But then she flashed another smile. "At least you can take your present. Naya mixed some water for you."

"Why would she do that, after she found out what I did to her?"

"Lucky for you, she made you the water before she found out." Bethany winked. She held the water bottle toward him.

He tried to reach for it but the shaking in his hand increased. He yanked his hand back again, afraid to spill the bottle and waste it.

Bethany set it down just outside the bars, within his reach. She skipped to the door of the dungeon floor. "See you around, Vass."

"Very funny."

~

August 29, Monday
Waxing Crescent

Whoever invented Monday must have been a demon. It rolled around just like a curse, before Naya was ready for it. She had to go back to work Monday morning, as if nothing had happened to her. No one else had shoved an extra year of their life into one day. No one else had fallen in love and had their heart broken in that same year of that one day.

For even though during most of the fake do-over day that they had spent together, Vass had wasted time spinning one lie after another, she also remembered the moments of naked need and honesty.

She remembers one day sandwiched in the middle of the year of repeat days when abruptly he told her the truth about everything. Not in a sneering, cruel way, but sadly.

He looked her in the eye and said, "You won't remember this because I've already decided this day is a bust. So I may as well tell you the truth. I've never been happier in my entire life than the time I've spent with you. It's been six months now for me and I'm falling in love with you. And by tomorrow, it will be today again, and you won't remember any of this."

"I'll remember finding you in the woods injured and healing you."

"Yes, okay, you'll remember that."

"And I remember you defending me from a Vampire outside the restaurant."

"Yes," he said, "You'll remember that. But you won't remember that I'm the one who made the Vampire who stalked you in the first place."

And she remembered saying to him, "There's a way you can make all of this right. Don't do over this day. Let time run forward. Accept your mistakes. Tell me you're sorry Wake up tomorrow. Don't erase this day. Don't pretend it didn't happen. Just move forward."

And she watched him walk away toward the truck.

At the time, she hadn't understood the significance of that, because he hadn't revealed to her how he altered time, but looking back on it now, she knew. He hadn't trusted her enough then to let her keep the memory of what he thought were his mistakes.

But then one day, he *did* let time go forward again. One day he just decided to start living for real. Over a year, he had fallen in love with her, but to her, he was still a stranger.

Now that she had the memories back, he wasn't a stranger anymore. Somehow, she had fallen in love with him. Not once, but many times, in a single day. It had been a fragile love, but compounded now by the restored memory, she realized it was not fragile any longer. She had seen him at his worst, and she had seen him at his best, and she was no longer afraid of him. She was only afraid of what he would do to himself.

She wished she could let him know that she didn't hate him. But it was too late. A year or a day, they'd spent all the time they would ever have together. She too could only go forward.

~

Bleary eyed and brokenhearted, Naya yawned her way up to lumberyard.

It wasn't yet 8 o'clock so the crews were milling around the yard waiting to drive up to the mountain and the timber. Riley walked up to her, clapped her on the back and grinned.

"You are one lucky boss, Naya," he said. "I was wondering what was going to happen now that Vass has been arrested."

"You heard about that?"

"We all heard. Turns out he stole that truck. Sheriff Lawson came by and was asking everyone questions about it. Too bad... for a Boar Shifter, he wasn't too bad. But you know what they say. Do the crime, do the time."

"Right." This must be the cover story the Guardians had decided to go with. Naya rubbed her eyes. "You said that there was some good news?"

"Gunner is back! So at least we'll have a dry kiln operator."

The Gargoyle flew down in his stone form, on wings of stone that should not have been able to carry him through the air, but magically did. He was carrying Sylvia in his arms as if she were blushing bride. She was also holding two ewers, the ones she had made for auditioning for Temperance.

Everyone congratulated Gunner for being back. He gave some explanation for why he had returned so soon, but he and Sylvia lingered in the yard after everyone else had gone to work for the day.

Once the three of them on alone, Sylvia said to Naya, "Actually Gunner never went to war. He also went to audition for Temperance."

Naya looked at him in surprise. Of course, it should've occurred to her that he qualified. He had Elemental Stone magic, naturally, since he was a Gargoyle, but as a rare additional skill, he also had Water magic. It was what made him such a good artist. There was a softer side to him that few people guessed looking at his hard muscular body and almost cruel-looking handsome face.

"I accepted the Call," he said. "I hope you're not angry, Naya. I know you were Called as well. But many are Called. Few accept. It's *whether you accept the Call* that matters."

"And as I told you before," said Sylvia. "There's a special requirement this time around." She put her arm around Gunner. "It turns out I was accepted as a Guardian as well, just not for the position I went in for. Gunner and I will ascend to the Guardianship together. He will be the new Temperance." She kissed his cheek. "He even looks the part part, doesn't he, with those wings?"

Sylvia shifted into her Faun form. She was wearing cut off Jean shorts, which did not hide her hairy goat legs at all. She grinned when Gunner brushed her thigh.

"My sexy little devil," he purred. "She is the new Pan."

Naya tried to hide her pain. She knew her pain arose from nothing but petty jealousy, not just for the Guardianship, but for the pure and true love they had found that enabled them to accept their new powers. If her love with Vass had been *true* love, then perhaps they would have... She cut the thought like a runny thread from the sweater that was unraveling.

"There's one other thing I want to tell you," said Gunner. "I did go to Autumndelle. I talked to your family there. They need you, Naya. I know you haven't been paying attention, but for the last ten years our homeland has been under the curse of Eternal Winter. The snows have finally started to melt now that we've pushed the Azir out, but the forest... They are devastated. So many trees died. They need you back home, to help them replant and regrow."

"With our new powers," added Sylvia, "we can help you move Quigley. You can go home, to your true home, to the forest of your mother and father and sisters and brothers and cousin dryads."

"But what about Timber Falls?"

"Sign that over to me, and I will be the new CEO," said Sylvia. "Gunner and I will run it together. Will still need cover stories for our human personas."

"Let's do that right now," said Gunner. "I know you can wallow in indecision for days, Naya. But we don't have time for that. We need to wrap this up before the end of August. Something important is happening in September."

"What is happening?"

"Guardian business." He smiled. "Sorry. I can't share that with you because you're not a Guardian."

"Let's go sign those papers," said Sylvia.

Naya followed them to her cottage. They sat down at the table in her dining room together. They had already put together an entire package of paperwork. There were places at the bottom of each page that she had to either sign or initial. They had even helpful he pointed them out with a little arrow stickers.

This all felt sickeningly familiar.

Twenty-Six

"JUST A MINUTE," said Naya. "I want to get a different pen."

She hurried into the spare bedroom. It still smelled masculine and savory and a little smoky, like Vass. She opened one of the drawers, pulled out a pen and a piece of paper and quickly wrote something on it. She signed her name. Then she placed the paper back into the drawer. She was going to take the pen with her, but then her gaze fell upon some boxes in the room. She had another idea.

Someone had sent the boxes, the four big wooden crates with her urns in them, to her house and she had shoved them into this back room for now. She opened two of them and mixed the waters. Then she decided to be certain and mixed the other two waters as well so that she had the potent healing potion. As a spell for general healing of any excess and restoring equilibrium, the Elixir of the Four Quarters had the ability to cast off some spells and illusions. It wasn't a strong as the touch from a Null, it did have restorative powers for both body and mind.

It was the only power she had.

She returned to the dining room and threw water onto both of her friends.

"Who are you really and what do you want for me?" Naya demanded.

Drenching wet and outraged, they leapt from the table and whirled to face her. Both of them were already in their Demi-human form, or they would've certainly changed. Gunner looked intimidating with his huge stone wings and massive stone muscles. Sylvia was very muscular as well, for a Faun, and her long horns were sharp. She lowered her head as if planning to gouge Naya's eyes out.

Naya's heart sank. She had hoped that these two wore only a Glamour, an illusion cast by some evil Elf, but they were real. The water would have washed away any mere Glamour.

However, the water did have some positive effect after all. The anger in them evaporated. Sylvia shook herself like a dog and Gunner rubbed his face.

"I don't know why we told you those lies..." Sylvia stammered. "Wait, yes, I do. I wanted to make you jealous. But Naya, none of it is true! We aren't Guardians!"

"I wanted it to be true," said Gunner. "I really did audition for Temperance as well. The Guardianship should have been mine...!" He shook his head again, as if throwing off another confused thought. "No, that's not true. I just wanted to make Sylvia proud."

For a moment they looked bewildered and ashamed, and Naya knew they were really her friends. But then the harsh, ugly sneers started to creep back onto their faces. They were under some compulsion much stronger than what her waters could wash away.

"We *do* deserve it," growled Sylvia. "And he said he would make it real."

"He did promise that we could fake it until we make it," said Gunner. "Why should we come in second place behind someone like you? You don't even have wings!"

"Sign the papers, Naya," ordered Sylvia.

"No."

The light in the room grew dim and then dark although it was only a little past eight on a summer morning that had started out bright.

Through the window, Naya could see that dark clouds had rolled overhead quickly. It looked like they were going to get one of those snap summer storms that made weather in Colorado so erratic and hard to predict.

The darkness outside made the kitchen and dining room of her little cottage even darker inside. Out of the shadows, a huge grotesque form solidified. She smelled fire and brimstone. The thing before her was fully demonic, and like Vass in his demon shape, it was an amalgamation of many different animals cobbled into the semblance of a man. But this body was corpulent in the extreme. And in addition to his fat, bristled swine legs the grotesque demon had tentacles coming out of his rib cage.

"There was an easy way to do this," said the fat, unctuous demon. "But you had to choose the hard way. Hold her down in the chair," he ordered.

As if hypnotized, Gunner and Sylvia obeyed him. They were both physically stronger than her, especially Gunner, whose vise-like hands were literally made from stone. While they pinned her to the chair, the hideous demon reached out for her with his tentacles. The slimy things wrapped around her arms, her legs, her waist, and her neck. Another tentacle started to crawl up her leg. She screamed and thrashed, trying to escape.

"You will soon *want* to obey me," he chuckled. "You will find pleasure in the pain I will bring you and you will beg to be my slave forever."

"Sylvia! Gunner! Please!"

"Get out of here!" the demon ordered the two people she had once called friends. "I don't need you anymore. This is now between me and my new pet."

～

August 29, Monday

Vass had told himself that he wasn't going to use the waters Naya prepared for him. But that was just his pride speaking. By halfway through Sunday evening, he was in so much agony that he drank the entire bottle. And yet, by Monday morning the symptoms were back. He curled up underneath the bed, as if hiding from the pain, but it came from deep inside him and nothing could protect him from it. The Chains felt like iron vises.

Memories flooded him. All of the worst moments of his life, including moments of his childhood that he had not remembered even happened until now. He suddenly saw that only a very small portion of his life had involved his father showering him with gifts and material pleasure. Those good times had been random, unpredictable, manipulative and based only on whether his father needed something from him at the time. The rest of his days, he had either been neglected or actively abused and humiliated for pleasure of those who were supposed to be caring for him.

One particularly painful memory was from when he was only five or six and desperately wanted to know who his mother was. His father told him that he would introduce her to him. A beautiful woman arrived at the mansion. She started out nice, showering him with cookies and candy. The food probably had dark magic in it, because he felt a weird compulsion to eat everything long after he felt full, even uncomfortably full. He kept eating and eating until he was so sick, he vomited. The woman who claimed to be his mother told him that he disgusted her, and she didn't want to be around him anymore. Then she left. His father returned and told him, "You see, Vass, I'm the only one you can depend on."

For years after that, he thought that was truly his mother. That he truly had disgusted her. That she left because he was unlovable. Later he found out she was just another demoness in his father's retinue, of no relation to Vass at all. She was an actress who frequently played roles like the one she had performed for his father.

Vass did eventually find his real mother. She was a dark magic addict and had no interest in him. By then he was much older, and expected nothing, so he wasn't as disappointed. And yet he had forgotten both of those memories until now that they came back to torture him.

Other memories tormented him as well, memories of all the ways he had messed up during the day he had lived over and over again trying to impress Naya. And he kept seeing the disgust on her face when she came to visit him in the prison. That replayed over and over again like its own do-over, but with no way to fix it.

He knew if he could FEED, then all of these memories would be erased from his mind again. Even if he could not be happy, he would once again feel pleasure. At least he would stop feeling pain.

The door to the dungeon opened. He groaned. As long as he was suffering from the Chains feeding on him with no way for himself to feed in turn, his captors did not even need to torture him. He was doing that all by himself. Maybe they just wanted to watch and gloat.

"Oh, it's just you," he said when he saw who it entered.

Bethany ran into the dungeon and grabbed the bars of his cage. Behind her, to his surprise, he saw the Faun, Sylvia... And that Gargoyle... wasn't that Gunner, the worker he had replaced?

"Vass!" cried Bethany. "Naya is in trouble. Some big fat demon is torturing her, trying to get her to sign some papers."

He roared and smashed his way out from under the bed overturning it as he switched to his full demon form. "That's my father! You have to let me out of here. I have to save her!"

"I don't have the key," said Bethany. "And there's no time to explain to the others why this is a good idea. They would probably tell me it's a very foolish idea."

"If there's no escape from this cage, why did you tell me this?"

"I'm touching the bars right now," she said calmly. "They are still iron, but the magic that protects them is gone as long as I touch them. I think in your demon form you can break iron, can't you?"

He didn't even wait to answer her. He just grabbed the bars and snapped them like twigs. Instantaneously he was free of the cage. He flapped his locust wings and disappeared from the Castle.

∽

Vass almost made the mistake of appearing in her cottage right away. At the last minute, it suddenly occurred to him that if he confronted his father still wearing the chains of hell, he would never free her. His father was probably attempting to chain Naya herself right now, a thought which drove Vass wild with fury, but he had to calm down and not rush into the situation where he would doom them both.

How can I free myself? He wondered. He remembered the meeting he had gone to with Michael. He could not do this on his own, he realized.

And so he appeared at the edge of the river near the waterfall where Naya said she had received her Calling. He didn't see any river goddess in the waters. He didn't hear any voice calling out sweetly to him that he had a higher destiny.

He waded into the water, until he was as deep as his chest. He closed his eyes. You, who created my soul, whoever you are, I say it belongs to you and no one else. Take it back. Please give me freedom so that I can help free the one I love. Then you can do whatever you want to me, I don't care.

A huge roar sounded like thunder in his ears. He looked up at the sky and saw that a storm had rolled overhead out of nowhere. Heavy rains poured out upon him, drenching the part of his body that was still out of the water. Lightning flashed overhead in the sky.

That was the answer to his incoherent prayer, he thought despairingly. He was going to be smited by lightning from the sky like the worthless evil worm that he was.

The rain was so heavy that even though it had just started, the water in the river began to rise. He realized that not all the thunder was coming from the sky. Above, on the slopes of the mountain, where the rain had already been falling for some time, the river was growing like a dragon gorging itself on a feast. And all of that water was pouring toward the falls. He started to scramble out of the way, but he could not make it. He sprayed his arms out wide and turned to face the waterfall. The huge wave of water crashed over the falls and washed over him, uprooting him from the riverbed and carrying him away downstream like a piece of flotsam.

~

Something wrapped around his body, securing him against the shore when the river would have washed him away. Vass grabbed hold and started climbing up. He had been caught in the roots of an ancient silver aspen tree. He climbed higher and higher until he was in the branches of the tree, above the floodwaters that drowned everything below him.

"Welcome," the tree said. It had a face. Vass almost fell out of the branches he was so surprised. "Yes, I can speak your language," said the tree. "When I need to. I am a Hamadryad. I know you. From Naya's heart. I am her best friend. And you are the one she loves."

Vass shook his head. "You are mistaken. She hates me."

"You can't argue with a tree," said the tree. "You are ready to fight for her now. She still in the cottage. Remember that nothing she is doing now is her own choice. Her love for you is the only thing that is real."

"I can't free her long as I wear to the chains my father put on me."

"What chains?" asked the tree. "You are free."

Vass was about to argue, and then he glanced down at himself. The tree was right. Vass was free of pain. And more importantly, he was free of the Seven Chains that had been bound to him in spirit. They were gone. Instead of the chains on his heart, his heart was protected by a ring of pure white light.

He snapped his fingers and reappeared in Naya's cottage.

The first thing he noticed were the sounds of sexual pleasure, animalistic grunts and groans. Then he saw her. She had her skirts kicked up wantonly to her waist, with her legs spread and wrapped around a fat man who was slobbering all over her neck in a grotesque imitation of kissing. He was licking her with a forked tongue. He had her pinned down, not only by his fat pudgy fingers but by multiple tentacles. And she had her head thrown back in apparent ecstasy. The demon ravishing her was Vass's own father, Xin Glug'ulgros.

Twenty-Seven

(New Day)

After a moment of rage that nearly blinded him and caused him to do something stupid, Vass forced himself to calm down and take in what was really happening. Whatever his father was doing to Naya had just begun. His father was still dressed, wearing a grubby tunic stained with food that was centuries out of date, probably because he had been wearing it without washing it ever since the Dark Ages.

The Demon King was about to rape Naya, but he hadn't gotten that far yet. He had only drugged her with dark magic and groped her with his slimy tongue and tentacles. It was disgusting enough, but Vass knew it would get much worse if he didn't fight his father now.

"Get away from her, father!" commanded Vass.

"Look at you," sneered his father. "Where did you get your shiny new halo?"

In any conversation with a demon like his father, the important thing was not to get distracted by any of his lies. Obviously, Vass did not have a halo. Vass ignored the taunt. He grabbed his father and yanked him away from Naya. He tried to transport both her and himself somewhere else, but his magic wasn't strong enough to overcome the dark gravity of his father's power. All he managed to do was throw Xin Glug'ulgros across the room so that the fat demon bounced off the stove like a giant rubber ball. The impact didn't even hurt the Demon King.

"I gave you every advantage," shouted his father. "I gave you every power! And this is how you repay me, you ungrateful worm!"

"You put chains on me to feed yourself!" Vass shouted back. "Do you think I don't know that the chains you locked on me went through YOU before they connected to the Infernal Machine? Do you think I don't know that you were trying to *feed on my energy* and that's the real reason you wanted me to harvest souls on earth? So that YOU could use me to feast on them yourself?"

"I came here to show you how it should be done!" sneered his father. He didn't respond to anything his son said. This was how their conversations always went, with no one responding to what the other one said, only shouting accusations: two parallel one-sided conversations.

His father showed images of Sylvia and Riley and Gunner. "You had vulnerable and delicious souls ready to be harvested right here where are you stationed yourself. Envy, lust, pride... It should have taken you only one day to suck their life force and seal this deal. And I don't mean one day with the help of a Sisyphus Engine!"

That was what demons called their own time repetition device. They had their own dirty and weaker imitation of the Chariot of Heaven. Apparently, Vass's father still had no idea that Vass has used the real thing and not the shoddy demon copycat version.

"I won't let you hurt the Dryad," Vass said.

"You're too late. I already have what I want." His father held up a stack of papers, which had been signed. "She signed away her property to me and she also signed away her soul. I own her now. Screwing her was just for fun. I still plan to do so, but I think I'll take both of you to Darkpyre first. I'll chain you to the wall and make you watch. If you beg, maybe I'll let you join us. We could take turns on her."

Vass's vision was blackening again. Whatever hold he had on the calm center he had found in the river, he could feel himself losing it. Wrath was building up in him and it was going to explode. He knew that was exactly what his father wanted, but Vass couldn't control himself any longer.

"You don't own me," said a deep feminine voice. It was Naya, but Naya as he had never seen her before. Her torn clothes no longer mattered, because she had switched to her Dryad form, and she wore a gown of bark. Her hair looked like golden autumn aspen leaves flowing down her back. Her eyes were the same, though. One brown and one green.

The papers that the demon king held in his hand crumbled into dust. He gaped. "That's not possible! You signed your name right in front of me!"

"But I had already signed a formal contract that invalidated that one." Naya looked at Vass. "I knew I would not be able to resist the dark magic of the King of Hell himself," she said, "So I had to give my soul to someone else first. Go look in the drawer in the room where you stayed. You will find it belongs to Vass already. No one else can have it."

Vass went into the room and found the paper. She had scribbled out the words, *"I give myself to Vassily Glug'ulgros as he gives himself to me. I am my beloved's and he is mine,"* and signed her name, Naya Fairchild.

It was a contract that required two signatures. She had placed all her faith in him, trusting that he would sign. If he refused, his father could still take her soul to hell.

He took the pen and signed his name as well. It was strange that although he had already given his soul to the Light, it was still his to give away again; and his soul was still his own, wholly and completely. Love was a strange form of attachment that multiplied instead of restricted and brought freedom instead of bondage.

He took the contract back and showed his father. Even the King of Darkpyre could not break a contract. The demons, too, had to follow the rules of the one who had created them, originally to be guardians of good, not evil, but with the ability to choose.

Of course, even though his father had to accept the contract it didn't mean he had to except it gracefully. He roared and shot fire out of his mouth.

"Excuse me," Vass said to Naya. "I have to kill my father now."

Vass turned into his demon form and with his boar tusks, he charged directly at him and shoved him out the door and halfway across the mountain.

The two monsters began to fight to the death.

Naya ran after them. The two demons had already flown so far in their feet battle that she could barely see them. It didn't help that the sky was almost as dark as night because of the summer storm that had rolled in and drenched everything with buckets of water. Lightning flashed and she saw the two demonic figures illuminated in the sky, grappling each other. Thunder crashed continuously, like cannons on a battlefield.

"You can't kill your own father," she screamed at him. "You'll undo everything that you've worked for!"

He gave no sign that he could hear her.

What could she do? Who could she turn to for help? Gunner could fly but he wasn't strong enough to stop either demon. Her own powers were in the water and on the land; she couldn't join the fight in the sky.

Suddenly she remembered Vass's "brother," Judge Renaci. She had seen him only once or twice in the do-over day, because he had kept himself hidden from her, but she knew about him. The Fallen Angel. She knew from the year of lost memories that the Fallen Angel kept a close watch on his friend even when it wasn't visible, as if he were still a guardian angel and not a creature of darkness. What was his full name?

"Raziel Renaci! Vass needs you!" she shouted. "RAZIEL! RAZIEL! HEY YOU DAMNED ANGEL! GET OVER HERE!"

And just like that, he appeared beside her. He looked strong and noble and yet tortured and torn at the same time. He had huge wings like those of a raven, but the feathers were broken and ratty.

"I want to help," the Fallen Angel said without preamble. He tried to lift his wing and showed that it had been broken and reset wrong and now could not spread. "But I can no longer soar."

"I can heal you wings," said Naya.

There was no time for the usual ceremonies. Naya pointed at the sky itself, at the rain pouring down. "Waters of the Four Quarters, heal this man and let him save my friend from his own wrath. Don't let him be lost again in the darkness of hatred."

Four portals opened in the sky and the rain from other Spheres poured on the Angel. Naya stirred them with waves of her hand mixing the waters so that the balancing properties of the waters restored the angel to his former glory. His wings became shiny black and healthy again. Raziel bowed his head and acknowledged her gift and then he sailed into the sky.

He didn't try to stop Vass as Naya had expected him to do. Instead, the dark angel opened a portal, grabbed the Demon King, and carried him through it. The portal winked out of the sky. Raziel and the Demon King were both gone.

August 30, Tuesday
(New Day)

Vass lifted his lips off of Naya's reluctantly when they both heard footsteps. He buttoned his shirt and Naya smooth her hair.

"There's not much privacy in a dungeon, is there?" she grumbled. "If it's not bad enough having a Vampire in the cell across from us, we seem to get visitors every five minutes."

"I'll see who it is," he promised. Someone had fixed the bed that he had knocked over the last time he left the cell. He closed the curtains around the four-poster bed, completely hiding Naya from view. He himself climbed out of bed and waited, standing up in the middle of the cell. If it weren't for the iron bars, the room compared to a comfortable hotel room. The matching cell across from this one was a little smaller and had less furniture, because until Yuri had been brought here by Chet, it had been uninhabited.

Yuri had a plain twin bed with sheets and blankets but no curtains. He sat on the edge of his bed and when he saw his former boss, Vass, staring at him between the bars, he snarled and turned his back to stare at the wall rather than talk to him.

Vass couldn't blame him. The Vampire had every reason to be furious. But the Guardians were not about to let the Vampire roam free when he was freshly minted and still unable to control his blood lust.

The big iron and silver laced door, heavy not only with the weight of its earthly components, but also with enchantments, opened ponderously at the far end of the large dungeon. The whole area taken all together was the size of a warehouse, although it only contained four cells altogether, two on either side of a broad walkway.

Michael and Chet entered the dungeon. They checked in briefly with the vampire, who only growled at them. Michael tossed Yuri a bag of blood.

"I can't eat that shit!" The Vampire hissed.

"Sorry," sneered Chet, "I'll just run out and grab a human off the street for you to drain."

The Vampire growled again, grabbed the blood bag, and sucked it dry.

Michael, meanwhile, walked close to cell where Vass stood.

"You came back," said Michael.

"Yes," confirmed Vass. He smiled ironically. "I locked myself up of my own free will. I prefer to think of it as rehab rather than prison."

"Just to make it clear... You *have* switched sides this time?"

"Yes," said Vass. "The Chains are gone. I can never go back, even if I wanted to."

"Not exactly the ringing endorsement I was hoping for," said Michael. "Where is Naya? I thought she was going to visit you. "

There was a chair in the hallway between the cells, well away from where a prisoner could reach with his arm. But the chair was empty.

Naya peaked her head out from within the bed curtains.

"I'm here," she said. Naya climbed out of the bed.

She was fully dressed in yoga pants and a T-shirt, but her hair still looked mussed, like they had just had sex. Which, of course they had. Wild, crazy, animal sex. They didn't even care that the Vampire could hear them. It was fantastic therapy, if he did say so himself.

She winked at Michael. "Just, you know, helping him to rehabilitate."

Michael blushed like a 15-year-old boy hearing his first dirty joke.

Vass laughed and Chet rolled his eyes. "You're such a choirboy sometimes, Michael. Did you find any sign of our mutual friend?"

His voice was heavy with sarcasm.

Michael shook his head. "No sign of Raziel. But I did see a huge lion in the woods when I was flying overhead. I think it might be Moxie's lost brother. We should send out hunters who can track on the ground better than I can from the air."

Michael returned his troubled gaze to Vass. "Is Raziel loyal to the Dark Triad?"

"Raziel hates the Dark Triad."

"Why didn't he return as soon as he was free—if you really freed him? And why did he save the life of the Demon King?"

"That's my fault," said Naya. "I know the Demon King deserves to die, but Vass doesn't deserve to stain his hands with the blood of his own father, no matter how terrible."

"So the idiot sacrificed himself for me—again." Vass grimaced. "Now he's probably enjoying my father's warm 'gratitude.' A slave again. If he survives, he'll be forced to serve the Dark Triad again. So my gesture was useless."

"Both of you need to come with us," said Chet. "The Council of Guardians has voted on what do with you, and you will now receive our verdict."

"Leave Naya out of this!" snarled Vass.

"Nope, sorry, she's tied to you now, Vass." Chet crossed her arms. "I'm afraid she's going to suffer the same fate as you."

Vass started to froth at the mouth, which made Chet smirk wider.

"You're enjoying this way too much, Chet," Michael chided.

Naya touched Vass's arm. "Let's see what they have to say, Vass. I'm not afraid."

~

They were taken to the same strange Portal (hidden in a large bank vault in a tower) that Naya had walked through before. All of the other Guardians were waiting in the tower room.

"Are we going to have to live through that year again?" Naya asked.

Vass looked horrified at the thought.

The Magician, who stood closest to the Portal, shook his head. "Not that. What happens next, however, depends on you two. Please hold hands and walk into the Portal."

Naya could feel Vass tense to fight. She could tell he assumed this was trick and something awful would be on the other side—torment, death, or worse, to him, humiliation. But Naya sensed no animosity from any of the Guardians. Their body language told her they were... expectant.

"Come, beloved," she said, and took his hand.

~

Together, Vass and Naya formally entered the Portal in the Castle Tower, walked through a tunnel of Light, a cathedral of light. At the center stood a round table of pearl and gold surrounded by twenty-two gleaming thrones.

Even Vass had heard this place described in legends and lore. It was the Temple of the Guardians.

Vass felt the same peace wash over him in that he'd felt when he surrendered his Chains in the river. Naya smiled at him, radiating joy. This feeling of contentment was the bliss he had always chased after in every addiction that had trapped him, and yet now he knew that all of those other false idols were nothing compared to the real feeling of love that he felt right now.

The other Guardians streamed into the Temple. All of them had obviously been here before. They seated themselves in thrones around both sides of the round table, filling up fourteen of the twenty-two thrones.

"Welcome *Sarmat* Vassily, *Sarmati* Naya," the Magician said formally. "Please take your seats. We must apologize for the haste, but we have business to conduct. We are unlikely to find all the Guardians before the Dark Triad strikes at the Mundane Sphere. We need every Guardian we can get on board."

Vass's jaw dropped.

Chet burst out laughing. "You thought you were giving up a throne, but look, you've got a much better one."

Vass and Naya had to separate, to sit on opposite sides of the table.

"From what Vassily has told us," said the Magician, "We know that the war is being driven by a Dark Triad of wizards. We know two of their names. King Xin Glug'ulgos and King Belliqas Izbognir. The third member is a mystery. We know that it was a member of the Dark Triad who Massacred the Guardians, but we don't know which one. They are going along with the war for their own reasons. We also know that the Dark Triad is building a Tower, that they intended to power with some kind of Super Weapon. Finally, we know the target date of their attack, perhaps the date they intend to detonate the Super Weapon: All Hallow's Eve."

The Seeress said, "I recently had a vision. One of the Guardians is going to betray us. One of the Guardians, and I don't know which, is going to help the murderer on the Dark Triad massacre the Guardians again."

Several Guardians turned troubled gazes to Vass.

Vass could guess the gist of their thoughts without needing to read minds.

"There's a reason I decided to lock myself back up," said Vass, seriously. "I broke the Chains, and I don't suffer from cravings anymore. But we all know the chances of an addict falling off the wagon again. Right now, I don't have any intention of ever going back to help my father, but what if something happens and I relapse?"

Naya declared, "If you fall, I'll pick you up again. We're in this together. You're not alone, Vass."

"We also have no reason to assume it would be you," said Michael generously.

"You do have a point," said Vass. "It could be Chet. He's a demon too, after all. Also, kind of an asshole."

"Eff off," said Chet.

"I rest my case," said Vass.

"It could be me," said Michael. "If Raziel fell from grace, why not another angel? The point is, it's probably going to be someone we least expect. That's who can do the most damage. But we can't start distrusting each other, we can't give into paranoia and suspicion. That's a sure way to create a self-fulfilling prophecy of betrayal from within."

"Don't forget," said Troy, the Emperor. "We don't even have all the Guardians gathered together yet. The traitor might not be among our ranks yet at all."

∼

The meeting went on some time. It felt surreal to Vass to be accepted as an equal councilor by those he had regarded as enemies until mere days ago.

After they left the Temple and returned to the Mundane Sphere to eat lunch in the Castle, Naya snuggled up to him.

"You don't really think that you will betray the Guardians?" Naya asked him. "You know that would be betraying me too. After all, you and I are both Guardians now. However unlikely it may seem to me, we belong here. Although I am very glad that I don't have to leave Timber Falls, since like everyone else I still need a cover persona for the human world."

"You *are* going to have to shift some responsibilities to your employees," he said.

"And I will," she said. "Maybe Sylvia and Gunner are not Guardians, but they are good people and powerful magic users. I do think they can take more responsibility if they are interested. If they aren't too ashamed of the way your father manipulated them to face me again."

He was still thinking about her question. "I don't want to ever betray you. But just because I've thrown off the chains once doesn't mean I won't just walk right back into them again. I've seen it happen before with other demons who tried to leave. I know it could happen to me. And I know you'll be there for me and maybe the other Guardians to, But...

"Sometimes I wake up in the middle of the night remembering things that just make me want to forget everything again."

She wrapped her arms around him.

"We will get through this. One day at a time."

If you enjoyed this book...

Please write a review on the site where you bought it. Even a line or two helps indie authors like me continue to bring you more novels to enjoy.

You can also write to me if you would like to tell me which character in this novella you would like to know more about! Several characters who appeared here are certain they will never fall in love, but the Light may have other plans.... Whose story would you love to read?!

If you liked this book, you will also enjoy the other novels and novellas set in Arcana Glen. These are all stand-alone Happily-Ever-After romances set in the Arcana universe, with recurring characters and an ongoing alternate history. Each series has an interconnected overarching story, but still has its own Heroine and Hero and happy, complete ending. Each book, even within a series, can be read and enjoyed independently.

Next up in the Major Arcana series is ***The Moon Bunny & the Sun Lion.*** As with all the Arcana Glen romances, this is a complete love story, but related to the ongoing quest to find all the new Guardians and the murderer who framed the Magician for the Massacre of the old Guardians.

Also check out the holiday novellas in the same universe. These shorter holiday-themed novellas in the Arcana Glen Cycle of the Year series can be read any time of year, just like any Arcana Glen novels.

Be sure and grab ***The Genie & the Gymnast***, a stand-alone Prequel sweet paranormal romance to The Major Arcana series.

Also by Tara Maya:

The Unfinished Song (Epic Fantasy):

- Initiate
- Taboo
- Sacrifice
- Root
- Wing
- Blood
- Mask
- Mirror
- Maze (September 2022)
- Sworn (Coming)
- Flute (Coming)
- Wheel (Final Book - Coming)

Arcana Glen Sweet Paranormal Romance Novels:

- The Magician & the Fool
- The Seeress & the Seraph
- The Dragon & the Slayer
- The Witch & the Warrior
- Moxie & the Maverick
- The Lawyer & the Leprechaun
- Death & the Detective
- The Demon & the Dryad
- The Moon Bunny & the Sun Lion
- The Tower & the Star
- Judgment & the World
- The Tree & the Egg

Arcana Glen Sweet Paranormal Holiday Novellas:

- The Genie & the Gymnast (available only here)
- The Tarot Reader's New Year Promise
- The Griffin's Fake Valentine Bride
- The Leprechaun's St Patrick Day Heist
- The Prodigal Wolf's Second Chance Easter Romance
- The Mermaid's Spring Fling Romance
- The Shifter's Best Friend at Beach Wedding
- The Sheriff's Magic Summer Jail Break

Science Fiction:

- Conmergence (short story collection)
- STRAT (Military Science Fiction)
- CIVIS (Strat Book 2 - Coming)

Books on Writing:

- 30 Day Novel: No Fail Formulas to Finish Your Novel

"Wow. Holy smoking wow. This is one of the few books I've read that I can honestly say was totally, 100% original.... However, as unique as it is, it was insanely easy to slip into the story..."

EMI LONDON, OCTOPUS INK

"I recommend this [series] ...to fantasy and epic saga lovers and readers who liked reading Lord of the Rings, but found the length of the book overwhelming....This book series has a unique concept - breaking down the traditionally long Epic Fantasy tale into shorter more manageable books."

GINA, MY PRECIOUS: RAMBLINGS OF A KINDLE
ADDICT

Start reading Initiate right now!

The Hot Dog Detective

BETRAYED BY HIS WIFE, *mocked by the man who murdered her, fired from the police department, MacFarland remakes himself as a hot dog vendor. But then a murder draws him back into the justice business...*

Betrayed by his wife and the system, former Denver Police Detective Mark MacFarland dropped out of the system...all the way. But now he has put drinking and homelessness behind him, bought a hot dog stand, and started a new life.

Then a noted defense lawyer asks MacFarland to prove that his client was wrongly accused of murdering her husband. Suddenly, MacFarland's past catches up with him.

Aided by his former partner, Cynthia Pierson, and his longtime homeless friend, Vietnam Vet Rufus, MacFarland discovers the husband's murder is actually part of a larger web of conspiracy...and may even tie in to the death of his wife.

. . .

Read the first book in this "cozy noir" mystery series for free.

Click here to read.